Bondi Beach Medics

Beachside rescues and sun-kissed romance!

With most of their childhoods spent roaming
Australia's shorelines with their nomadic parents,
Sydney was the only place that the Carlson siblings
made their home.

And now they're back! Living under the same roof
and practicing the medicine they love. Saving lives
in its hospitals and on its beaches. After all, they
never could resist the call of the surf!

Yet as the familiar embrace of Bondi Beach's
coastline welcomes them in life and career,
it's the call of love that could truly make this place
their home.

Discover Poppy's story in
Rescuing the Paramedic's Heart

Read Jet's story in
A Gift to Change His Life

Check out Daisy's story in
The Perfect Mother for His Son

Don't miss Lily's story in
Marriage Reunion in the ER

All available

D1025432

Dear Reader,

This is the fourth and final book in my Bondi Beach Medics series.

Lily, the eldest of the four Carlson siblings, returned to Bondi from London after a life-altering event, leaving her husband, Otto, behind. Lily is an emergency doctor and gorgeous Otto is a trauma surgeon, but they need to find a way to overcome trauma of their own in order to rebuild their life together.

I'm sorry to say goodbye to Carlson siblings Lily, Jet, Poppy and Daisy, and their lives in Bondi. I have really enjoyed the chance to tell their stories, to see them support each other, succeed in their professions and find love. I hope I have delivered on my promise of drama, adversity, love and laughter set against a backdrop of sun, surf and summer at Australia's busiest and most famous beach.

The other titles in the series are *Rescuing the Paramedic's Heart*, *A Gift to Change His Life* and *The Perfect Mother for His Son*. All are available as books and ebooks from your favorite retailer.

I'd love to hear from you if you've enjoyed this story or any of my others. You can visit my website, emily-forbesauthor.com, or drop me a line at emilyforbes@internode.on.net.

Emily

MARRIAGE REUNION
IN THE ER

———

EMILY FORBES

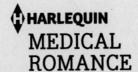

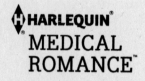

HARLEQUIN®
MEDICAL
ROMANCE™

Recycling programs
for this product may
not exist in your area.

ISBN-13: 978-1-335-73740-3

Marriage Reunion in the ER

Copyright © 2022 by Emily Forbes

All rights reserved. No part of this book may be used or reproduced in any manner whatsoever without written permission except in the case of brief quotations embodied in critical articles and reviews.

This is a work of fiction. Names, characters, places and incidents are either the product of the author's imagination or are used fictitiously. Any resemblance to actual persons, living or dead, businesses, companies, events or locales is entirely coincidental.

For questions and comments about the quality of this book, please contact us at CustomerService@Harlequin.com.

Harlequin Enterprises ULC
22 Adelaide St. West, 41st Floor
Toronto, Ontario M5H 4E3, Canada
www.Harlequin.com

Printed in U.S.A.

Emily Forbes is an award-winning author of Medical Romance for Harlequin. She has written over thirty-five books and has twice been a finalist in the Australian Romantic Book of the Year Award, which she won in 2013 for her novel *Sydney Harbor Hospital: Bella's Wishlist.* You can get in touch with Emily at emilyforbes@internode.on.net, or visit her website at emily-forbesauthor.com.

Books by Emily Forbes

Harlequin Medical Romance

Bondi Beach Medics

Rescuing the Paramedic's Heart
A Gift to Change His Life
The Perfect Mother for His Son

London Hospital Midwives

Reunited by Their Secret Daughter

Falling for His Best Friend
Rescued by the Single Dad
Taming Her Hollywood Playboy
The Army Doc's Secret Princess

Visit the Author Profile page
at Harlequin.com for more titles.

CHAPTER ONE

Lily looked around the almost empty bedroom at the bare walls and the pile of linen
that had been stripped from the bed and
dumped in the middle of the mattress. Daisy's possessions had been packed into boxes,
ready to be moved to her fiancé's house at
the other end of Bondi Beach, and for the
first time in two years Lily would be alone
in her house.

She hadn't stopped to think about how she
was going to feel but seeing the barren room
with all traces of her little sister removed
was confronting. It signalled the end of an
era. An end she wasn't ready for. She'd never
lived here without company. She was happy
for Daisy, of course she was, she'd found her
person and was heading off to start a new
life, but the empty room looked so final. So
lonely.

Lily and Daisy had both made their choices,

although the outcomes were very different, and for Lily her choices meant she'd have to get used to being alone.

She was an adult, she could manage, she reminded herself. She should be looking forward to having a whole house to herself, it was something she'd never experienced, but she was worried it wouldn't be to her liking.

She'd grown up sharing a bedroom with another sister, Poppy. Until the age of eighteen when she'd moved to Sydney to study medicine they'd shared a room, clothes and dreams. When Lily had moved into university accommodation, she'd still shared common spaces, if not a bedroom, with dozens of other students. She'd only moved out of there when she'd got married.

As a child she'd longed for a room of her own, space of her own. She should be looking forward to this next chapter, but she was acutely aware of the hole Daisy's departure was going to leave in her life. The hole Lily had filled by caring for her siblings. But all three of them were making their own way in the world now, forging ahead with their futures. They didn't need her any more and she didn't know how she would fill that gap without anyone to mother, without anyone to fuss over.

As the eldest of the four Carlson siblings she had always mothered her younger brother and sisters. Lord knew their parents hadn't been interested in raising their own kids, so Lily had taken on that role more often than not. She should enjoy having no one to think about but herself, she should be looking forward to this next chapter, but she could already feel the weight of her loss and her past decisions weighing her down.

She hoped they weren't going to crush her.

Too much time on her own would leave her with too much time to think and she knew where her mind would wander.

To Otto.

'Is that everything?' Daisy's fiancé's voice interrupted Lily's thoughts and she turned her attention away from the past and back to what was going on around her.

Daisy nodded. She'd been taping the last packing box closed but she'd stopped what she was doing to look at Ajay.

'What about that one?' Ajay asked as he pointed at a flat white box perched on the top shelf of the wardrobe.

'That's not mine,' Daisy replied as Lily's heart skipped a beat. She hadn't looked inside that box for years but she knew exactly what it contained.

Daisy stood up and started to shove her bed linen into a large bag as Ajay picked the final box up from the floor. He waited until she was looking at him again. Mindful of her hearing impairment he made sure Daisy could read his lips, before he asked, 'I'll take this to the car and wait for you there if you're ready to go?'

Daisy nodded again before turning to face Lily. 'Are you sure you don't want to come to us for dinner?' she asked.

'I'm sure,' Lily replied. She knew the house was going to feel empty but Daisy was heading off to her new life, off on a new adventure with her fiancé and his son, Niki, and Lily didn't want to intrude. She would find something to occupy her time, something to keep her mind engaged, something to enable her to ignore the quiet solitude because she knew she wouldn't enjoy it.

She pasted a smile on her face as she hugged her sister and Ajay and waved them goodbye before returning to Daisy's old bedroom intending to remake the bed. Perhaps that would help it to look less lonely. Less empty. As long as she could ignore the indentations in the carpet where Daisy's chair and chest of drawers had been she might be able to pretend someone still occupied that room if the bed was made.

She crossed the room, intending to get the spare linen out of the wardrobe, but her attention was drawn to the white box that sat on the top shelf, taunting her. She reached out, planning to slide the wardrobe door closed, to put the box and its contents out of her mind. She'd make the bed another time, she decided. But instead of hiding the box away she found herself reaching for it and taking it off the shelf.

She sat on the bed and lifted the lid.

She brushed her hand over the tissue paper that lined the box. It crinkled under her fingers, daring her to remove it.

She knew this was the last thing she should be doing when her nerves were already stretched tight, when the loneliness was like a demon hiding in the shadows daring her to look his way.

If she ignored the shadowy corners in her mind, if she kept her gaze averted, her attention diverted, she could keep the demon at bay, but she wasn't strong enough.

She pulled the top sheet of paper off and ran her fingers over the fabric that had been hidden underneath, feeling the tiny, delicate, fabric flowers that were scattered over the material, separating the individual petals from one another.

She slid one finger under the folds of milky white fabric that lay beneath the flowers. Despite the warmth of the late summer evening the satin was cool to touch.

She knew she should resist temptation. She knew she should put the lid on the box and hide it away again. The past was the past, there was no going back.

But her hands weren't listening. They were working independently of her mind. She intended to pick up the tissue paper, to layer it back in the box but instead she hooked her fingers under the narrow straps of fabric and lifted the contents from the box.

She stood up with the straps looped over her fingers, as the skirt of the dress fell to the floor.

Lily stepped in front of the mirror and held the dress up against her.

The smooth satin of the skirt brushed over her bare legs as it hid her shorts. She swayed slightly and the satin swished over her hips. She pressed her hands tightly to her shoulders, holding the dress to her body, making sure she wasn't tempted to try it on. She knew it would still fit her but she had no intention of wearing it again. Anxiety, skipped meals and an occasional break from work to go surfing had kept her weight constant and her figure was pretty much unchanged from the last, and only, time she'd worn this dress. On her wedding day almost five years ago.

She took a deep breath and closed her eyes as the memories flooded back.

She and Otto had been married for nearly five years but it had been two years since she'd last seen him, since she'd said goodbye, and somewhere along the way even their conversations had dwindled to discussions about the house they owned, their jobs on opposite sides of the world and the weather.

She could blame the time difference or their busy lives for their lack of communication but if she was honest she knew she'd avoided picking up the phone in an attempt to block out the past, to block out the reason she'd left.

She had never imagined their relationship would deteriorate so badly. What did that mean for their future? Did they even *have* a future?

She'd thought Otto would come after her but, when he hadn't, she'd gradually begun to reimagine her life solo. That hadn't been her intention initially but now it looked as if it was the only way forward. She'd avoided

Otto, avoided the difficult conversations, avoided talking about their loss. She knew it was too painful for her to broach that subject but she had no idea if Otto was as afraid of that conversation as she was or whether he was just oblivious to her pain. To her sadness.

She knew Otto was an optimist. He looked on the bright side of life—always looked for the positives, was always in good spirits. His attitude had always been 'why worry about the things you couldn't change' and he chose to focus his energy on the things he could control.

Otto had always been much more carefree while Lily was more serious. His personality had been a good foil for hers. Until one day when their differences had collided with each other instead of complementing each other.

Until the day that Lily's dreams of a perfect life, of children and a family of her own, had been shattered.

She wasn't pessimistic by nature but her positivity had taken a beating. She'd been distraught but Otto hadn't understood her devastation. His mantra was 'what's done is done, move on, put it behind you'. His life hadn't stopped, his focus hadn't wavered.

He'd forged ahead on his path, insistent that they'd get past the loss. But she hadn't been able to. And one loss had led to another.

She hadn't been able to handle Otto's lack of support. She'd felt unsupported, misunderstood and miserable. And so she'd walked away.

She'd lost everything.

She opened her eyes, turning her back on the mirror, not wanting to look at the dress. It was a symbol of a future she no longer had.

She'd learned to compartmentalise her memories. She'd locked them away. It was the only way she'd been able to get through each day. She'd wanted to talk to Otto but they had barely spent any time together after the incident. No, she needed to call it what it was—the assault. It was two years ago but she hadn't yet forgiven Otto for not keeping his word. If Otto had come home when he should have, she wouldn't have been assaulted and they wouldn't have lost their baby.

She had been more than five months pregnant at the time. She'd survived morning sickness, homesickness and immense fatigue all while starting a new job and had reached the point where she'd been enjoying the pregnancy and was excited about the future. She'd known Otto had been less ex-cited, the pregnancy hadn't been planned, advancing their timeline, but she was certain he'd change his mind once he held his child in his arms. She delighted in reaching the milestones, in feeling her baby kick. Feeling the hiccoughs and watching as her stomach moved and stretched as the baby performed somersaults in her womb. She'd lain awake at night, uncomfortable but happy, dream-ing of the life they would have, their family of three, and had been convinced it would all work out just as she pictured.

And then it had all gone wrong.

She knew it wasn't all Otto's fault. The blame lay with the man who had assaulted her, who had punched her in the stomach, stolen her bag and left her lying on the ground as he'd run off. But if Otto hadn't changed his plans, if he'd left work when he was supposed to, she wouldn't have been in the wrong place at the wrong time. She wouldn't have lost their baby.

Anger had become intertwined with her sadness, leaving her feeling bereft, adrift and alone. Unsettled and upset, she'd fled Lon-don, leaving Otto and their marriage behind. After two years she'd learnt to put the past aside in order to face each day. She hadn't forgotten what had happened but she was learning to live with it.

Forgiveness was a different story. She knew it was important but it was something she had struggled with. Perhaps one day she could learn to forgive if not forget.

She sighed. She hadn't wanted to give up on her dreams, on the idea of marriage and a family, but it was time she faced facts. Her marriage was over.

She didn't have to completely give up on her dream of a family but it was time to acknowledge that her dream was going to look different, *had* to look different. She could have a family but it wouldn't be with Otto.

She still wanted that perfect life and while she might not be able to change the past it didn't mean she had to give up on her future.

She folded her wedding dress and put it back into the box, covering it again with the tissue paper. For a brief moment she thought about seeing if either of her sisters wanted to borrow it. They were both engaged but while it would fit Poppy it would be too big for Daisy and was it bad luck to borrow a wedding dress from a marriage that hadn't lasted?

Technically Lily and Otto were still married, but her marriage and her life were in limbo.

It was time to face facts—Otto wasn't coming back.

In the back of her mind she'd always expected that he would come for her and she'd kept extending the timeline in her head. She'd made excuses: he was busy—working and studying for his fellowship, they'd been living on opposite sides of the world and the global pandemic had made travel to Australia from London all but impossible. But Otto's fellowship was due to finish this month, international travel was back on the agenda and there was still no sign of him coming home.

She wondered what his plans were. Surely he would have told her if he was coming back to Australia? He had Italian parentage on his mother's side, he could decide to stay overseas, and the fact he'd said nothing made her think he was settled in England, that he'd given up on them. On her.

If he wasn't coming back she had two options. She could go to him or she could move on without him.

She still loved Otto. She'd never stopped loving him. But she'd blamed him for failing to protect her. He'd promised to look after her, she'd trusted him to do that but he'd let her down.

She knew she wasn't blameless either, she'd failed to protect their child and that knowledge had been hard to accept and she knew it had contributed to the situation she found herself in now. She knew she'd run away. She hadn't been able to cope with seeing Otto every day. He had been a reminder of her broken dreams. They should have been able to help each other but instead all Lily had felt was a gaping divide between her emotions and his, her needs, her feelings, her hopes and dreams and his.

And she hadn't been able to bring herself to return to London, to go back to Otto. She still struggled to comprehend how their fairy tale had gone so wrong. The past two years had seen them drift further and further apart until she felt as if there was nothing left any more. And, while they lived on opposite sides of the globe, she knew their problems were unsurmountable.

Should she go back now? Give their marriage a chance?

Without realising, she shook her head. Since the day she'd announced her unexpected pregnancy it was clear they were on differing timelines and nothing had changed.

Otto would have told her if he wanted a family now. She would have told him if she was prepared to wait. It was that simple.

It had taken her some time to come to terms with the loss of their first baby but she had never wavered from knowing she wanted to be a mother and the unexpected pregnancy had only made her want that sooner rather than later. And now that her siblings were all settling down her biological clock was ticking overtime. In the past few months her brother and two sisters had all found true love and Lily had been left reassessing her own future. Otto had stopped asking about her plans a long time ago but it was clear in her heart, if not her head, what she wanted. She wanted a family. It was that simple.

She had to move on.

She couldn't go back.

She couldn't face returning to the place where it had all gone wrong.

She'd failed him but he had failed her too. He'd let her down, he'd lost her trust and she didn't know if he could win it back again. Or if he even wanted to.

She had wondered if they would ever be able to resolve their issues but the more time that passed, the more unlikely that seemed.

In her head she knew it was too late for their marriage. Surely if they were meant to be together they would have found their way back to each other by now.

What was left to fight for? What was easier to give up? Otto or her dreams of having a family? What was more important?

Her heart ached but she knew the answer. It was time to move on. The time had come to move forwards.

She put the lid on and slid the box back onto the shelf, relegating her wedding dress to her past, the decision made but not made lightly.

She shut the wardrobe door and checked the time. It would be mid-morning in London. She and Otto needed to have a frank discussion but she couldn't call now. He would be at work but even if he answered the phone she wouldn't know what to say. She needed time to prepare.

She would delay for one more day. What difference would a day make now after two years? She'd use the time to make some notes, to sort through her thoughts, to prepare her argument.

There was a lot to resolve but it was beginning to look as though it would be better just to start again. She'd waited long enough.

She wiped a tear from her cheek with the back of her hand as she closed the bedroom door. It was time to take a leaf out of Otto's book and do something about the things that were under her control.

Otto was woken by the flight attendant serving his breakfast accompanied by the pilot's announcement that they were on schedule for their arrival into Sydney. He stretched his shoulders and adjusted his seat as he tried not to think about how much he'd paid for his spot in business class. He'd slept well, the expense had been worth it and if he was going to worry about the price he shouldn't have booked the fare. He could afford it. There were probably other things he could have done with his money, there always would be, but the ticket was paid for, what was done was done, and he wasn't going to feel guilty about the extra luxury and comfort.

He'd been raised to work hard. To save money, to not live beyond his means, to be charitable. Money wasn't for frivolous things. His upbringing had been religious, nothing extreme, but he and his brothers had been taught to look after others, to be charitable.

His mother had always made them put

their own money on the plate at church, she'd instilled in them the importance of giving back. She had died when Otto was thirteen but he continued to be charitable as a way of honouring her memory. He still missed his mother but it was what it was. He'd learnt not to wish things were different, not to worry about the things he couldn't change. That mindset had come about as a direct reaction to his mother's death, a defence mechanism. He realised that wishing she hadn't been on the road at the same time as a drunk driver wasn't going to bring her back and so he'd learnt to worry about what he could control. To fix the things he could.

He shook out his napkin and tucked into his breakfast. Flying business class was a luxury but he refused to add more guilt to his conscience. He had enough already.

He'd worked non-stop for the past two years and he needed to take a break and if the only break he was going to get was on a long-haul flight from London to Australia that would have to do. Working hard had been a choice, a deliberate measure to combat loneliness. Finding himself with time on his hands—time he hadn't wanted—he'd filled those hours by studying, working and volunteering for extra shifts, offering to work on all the holidays, including Christmas.

Keeping occupied had served its purpose. It had left him with no time to think about anything other than medicine but he'd reached a crossroads and he needed to take stock of his life, to work out what he wanted to do next.

He could have stayed in London, he'd been offered a position in the hospital there, but he'd also been offered a position at Bondi General, replacing a surgeon who was retiring. Receiving an invitation to his sister-in-law's wedding had been an added persuasion, the extra push he needed to set a date to get on the plane. But even without that, when he weighed up his options, he knew he only had one choice. He had to come home. There was one thing he had to prioritise above all else.

His marriage.

That was assuming he still had one.

He hadn't seen his wife in almost two years. For the past seven hundred and eight days he and Lily had had a marriage in name only. They'd shared nothing but phone calls since Lily had packed her bags and walked out of their London flat.

He hadn't tried to stop her from leaving.

She'd told him she needed to go and he'd believed her. But he'd never intended to let her go for good.

Living on the opposite side of the world from his wife during a pandemic wasn't ideal and the time difference and their busy schedules hadn't conspired to make it easy. Their phone conversations had been brief, superficial and never particularly satisfactory and the calls had become progressively shorter, less frequent and less revealing.

Now, he had no idea what she was thinking. When they were first married they'd spent hours talking about their hopes and dreams but all of that had changed after Lily left. They never discussed their feelings in their phone calls and he wasn't sure how she felt about him, their marriage, their past or their future now. Had the passage of time healed her wounds? The loss of their baby had affected her deeply. It wasn't something they talked about at great length but he knew she'd taken it hard. Should he have encouraged her to talk to him about it?

He knew he hadn't because he didn't want to upset her and because he didn't want to see the accusations in her eyes. He'd felt guilty. His actions had put her in a vulnerable position. He hadn't been the one to cause her physical harm but the emotional injuries had scarred Lily just as badly and he still felt guilty.

Would time have healed the wounds? Would she have forgiven him? Would she be happy to see him?

He'd felt so confident when he'd been making plans to return to Australia. He had visions of what his future would look like. But as the plane flew over the Australian continent he began to wonder if he was wrong.

He wasn't sure he believed that absence made the heart grow fonder. His feelings for Lily hadn't changed in the past two years, they'd always been powerful. He'd remained faithful to her, he had made a promise to her on their wedding day five years ago and it was a promise he intended to keep. But he didn't know if Lily would have done the same. Had their separation changed her? Maybe there was a time limit on absence.

He hadn't been able to fix her two years ago. She'd been broken and he'd had no idea how to put her back together. After losing the baby there was so much they'd never spoken about. Where did that leave them?

Two years was a long time. Was it too long? The loss of their baby had torn them apart. Did they have the tools to put the relationship back together? Did Lily want him back?

He hadn't told her he was coming back and he knew it was because he'd been afraid she might have told him not to bother.

His trepidation grew as breakfast was cleared and his arrival was imminent. He wondered what sort of welcome he was going to receive. Would Lily be pleased to see him?

He felt the descent begin and he looked out of the window at the city as the plane approached the airport. It was a glorious summer's day, the harbour shimmered under the sun's rays and the iconic bridge stretched over the water, curving against the blue sky.

He was home.

CHAPTER TWO

'LILY, INCOMING AMBULANCE. ETA three minutes. Male cyclist, hit by a car. Can you take that one?'

Lily nodded as the triage nurse raced past with instructions. She was treating a child who was suffering from heat exhaustion. He was dehydrated and had been vomiting but fortunately his temperature was not elevated into an alarming range. She finished setting up the IV fluids and quietly instructed the nurse to stay with the patient and to be alert for any seizures. She peeled off her surgical gloves and apron and exchanged both for fresh protection. The ED at Bondi General was busy and she knew it was a juggling act trying to prioritise their patients. School had returned after the summer holidays but the February heatwave continued to see people flocking to Bondi and the surrounding beaches and when things went wrong those same people came through the ED doors.

Lily's first thought was why did someone feel the need to go for a bike ride when the mercury was nudging a hundred degrees Fahrenheit?

The ambulance pulled into the bay. She recognised the paramedic who climbed out of the back as one who often worked with her sister Poppy.

'Hi, Alex, what have we got?' she greeted him as he pulled the stretcher from the ambulance.

'Fifty-two-year-old male cyclist, multiple injuries. LOC, right upper limb fractures, rib fractures, abrasions, lacerations. BP one hundred over sixty. Pulse ninety-eight. He's in and out of consciousness. GCS of eight.'

The cyclist's helmet, what was left of it, was tucked at his feet. He was fortunate that he'd been wearing one—without it, Lily suspected he might have been taken straight to the morgue.

Her initial thought about the ridiculous decision to go for a ride in this heat was replaced with another, more pressing thought given the seriousness of the patient's injuries. His injuries were extensive and as she and Alex pushed the stretcher inside she knew he was going to need more skills than she could offer.

'We're going to need a trauma surgeon,' she said to Julie as she and Alex pushed the patient into the ED and headed directly to a treatment room.

The patient was transferred to a bed and the ED team got to work. Nursing staff inserted cannulas to run drips and attached him to the monitors. Lily kept one eye on his vitals as she prioritised his injuries. His BP had dropped further and she wondered if he had internal injuries with associated undetected internal bleeding.

'Can someone organise to cross-match blood type and run some O negative now?'

Lily picked up a torch and checked his pupils for reaction to the light, starting her assessment at the head, deeming that the most critical and planning to work her way down his body.

His eyes remained closed when she finished, no response to verbal stimuli but as they didn't know his name that made things difficult. She applied pressure to his fingertip, squeezing firmly, and was relieved to see his eyes flicker open. The door opened as she released his hand.

'All right, someone catch me up.'

That voice from behind Lily was so familiar. It brought goosebumps to her skin and made her catch her breath. A silly reaction, she knew it couldn't be Otto. Her ears were playing tricks on her—she was imagining Otto's voice because he'd been in her thoughts.

She glanced over her shoulder to see who she'd mistaken for Otto and almost dropped the torch.

Her husband was standing inside the doorway.

'Otto!' Lily felt the blood rush from her head, making Otto's face swim before her eyes. She put one hand out, reaching for the bed to support herself as her vision blurred and her legs threatened to fold beneath her.

'Hello, Lily.'

Lily could feel her eyes bugging out of her head as her brain tried to catch up with what she was seeing. Her husband, who as far as she'd been aware was supposed to be on the other side of the world, was standing in front of her.

She squeezed her eyes shut for a moment, clearing her mind, half expecting when she opened them that he would have disappeared. Half expecting that she was imagining things.

But no, he was still there, in her ED.

She opened her mouth wanting to ask what he was doing, why he was here, but her powers of speech deserted her.

'Everyone, this is Dr Rodgers, our new trauma specialist.' Julie was standing beside Otto, introducing him to the team.

Lily snapped her jaw shut, closing her mouth, waiting for her world to stabilise, hoping Julie wouldn't ask how they knew each other but fortunately there was no time for idle chat, they had a critically ill patient to manage.

Lily found her voice, and she could hear herself recounting the patient's history and assessment so far. Her head was spinning and she hoped she was making sense as she tried to process what was happening. No one corrected her summary so she assumed she must be giving the correct information.

Otto was standing beside her. She could feel the warmth emanating from his body, making her skin tingle. She wanted to look at him, still unable to believe what she was seeing, but she kept her eyes fixed on the patient, knowing she'd likely lose her train of thought completely if she looked Otto's way.

'GCS was eight,' she said as she watched one of the nurses removing road gravel from where it was embedded in the patient's upper arm. The cyclist had been wearing a short-sleeved Lycra riding suit, which was now dirty and torn and hadn't afforded him much protection against the metal of the car that hit him or against the hot bitumen of the road where he would have eventually come to rest. Lily kept her focus on those small deliberate movements as she spoke, ignoring the fact her husband—estranged, absent, she didn't know what to call him—was standing beside her. 'Blood pressure is still dropping. I'm worried about internal injuries. He's going to need scans.'

'Lily!' The nurse opposite her lifted her head, pausing her task to get Lily's attention.

The road gravel had packed a laceration, stemming the blood loss, but as the nurse had removed it the wound had opened up and blood was gushing from a now gaping hole. In a matter of seconds, the sheet was soaked in blood.

'Lacerated brachial artery. I need a tourniquet and an operating theatre. Now!' Otto shouted as the alarms on the monitors started beeping.

Lily grabbed a tourniquet and tightened it around the patient's arm as one of the nurses picked up the phone and called Theatres.

'You can use OR Three,' the nurse said as she hung up the phone and began to disconnect the monitors from the wall.

Lily checked that the tourniquet had stopped the blood loss before pulling up the cot sides. Otto had already kicked the brakes off and had moved to the head of the bed. There was no time to wait for an orderly with a bed mover.

'Let's go,' he instructed. 'Lily, keep an eye on that arm, make sure that tourniquet stays tight.'

Otto was already moving, pushing the bed in front of him, obviously expecting Lily to accompany him.

Adrenalin surged through her as she half walked, half ran, beside the bed, steering it out of the ED and towards the lift where one of the nurses was holding the door open for them.

They manoeuvred their patient into the lift. Lily squeezed in next to the wall and pressed the button for the operating floor. The doors slid closed and all of a sudden it was just her, Otto and their unconscious patient.

Otto had squeezed himself in next to Lily and she moved further into the corner, putting as much distance between them as she could. She gripped the rails on the bed side, grounding herself as she stared at him.

She couldn't believe he was back.

She couldn't believe he hadn't told her.

She felt ambushed. If she'd learnt one thing from her chaotic childhood it was that she coped best if she had a chance to prepare. She dealt in knowns, not unknowns. Even when working in the ED she dealt in facts, she knew the science. Years of study had taught her what to look for, she understood the signs and symptoms and they indicated how to treat her patients. She was always prepared. Always. But not today. His arrival had caught her by surprise and as she thought about his unannounced appearance her shock turned to anger. How dared he not let her know?

She was about to castigate him when the lift stopped. The operating theatres were only one floor above the ED and the short ride had saved Otto from a verbal tirade.

He reached out for the rail on the bedside as the doors slid open, his hand coming to rest on top of hers. The heat of his touch burned through her, searing her skin. She yanked her hand away as the theatre staff pulled the bed out of the lift and whisked the patient away. Otto followed them, issuing instructions, not even glancing Lily's way before he disappeared, leaving her alone.

Everything had happened so quickly and to find herself standing in the corridor alone was disconcerting. She leant on the wall for a moment, sifting through her feelings and recovering her equilibrium. She was astounded, confused and annoyed.

His return had completely blindsided her and the fact that he hadn't bothered to tell her he was coming home reinforced that she'd been right to start thinking about moving on. He'd shown her no regard. He hadn't warned her. He hadn't made time for her. He hadn't even looked back at her just now. He'd just walked away.

She had no idea why he was back or what his return meant but she intended to stick to her plan. She couldn't let his reappearance disrupt her. She needed someone who would support her when the going got tough. Life wasn't easy, she knew that all too well, and she deserved to have someone who had her back.

She returned to the ED and picked up her phone from the triage desk. She needed to get on top of things and put her plan in place.

Her hand was shaking as she typed in a message.

We need to talk.

The text was simple and unemotional and nothing at all like she felt but she had to keep her emotions in check. She'd made a decision.

She hit 'send'.

Otto turned the shower on full, letting the needles of water pepper his skin. He rolled his shoulders and felt the tension of the day and the fatigue of jet lag leave his body. It had been a stressful start to his new role.

His first official day had gone as expected professionally but not emotionally. After two years apart his intention had been to see Lily in private before he started work. He'd called her when he landed yesterday but her phone had gone straight to voicemail. He'd assumed she was at work and he'd left a simple message saying he'd call again later before jet lag had caught up with him.

Seeing her at the hospital today had thrown him off balance. He realised he hadn't mentally prepared himself for the possibility that he'd run into her at work first. A stupid oversight, he knew now. She was an ED doctor, he was a trauma surgeon, it was highly likely they would cross paths at work but he hadn't really considered that scenario. In his head, he had a vision of how their reunion would go and having it at work hadn't been the picture he'd conjured. It had thrown him. And it had obviously unsettled Lily.

He closed his eyes and put his face under the spray as he thought about the text message she'd sent him this afternoon.

We need to talk.

It was brief, hard to decipher. It felt terse but perhaps she'd sent it in a hurry. He found it difficult to read the tone of a text message at the best of times. No emojis, no clue. All he had to go on was her reaction to him when he'd appeared in the ED. Surprise. Shock. Both of which were to be expected given the circumstances. It wasn't an ideal start to his planned reunion and he owed her an apology for appearing out of the blue. He wouldn't call her. He needed to see her.

He walked to the shops, picked up a couple of things and then hailed a taxi.

The drive took him past Bondi Beach where the late afternoon sun turned the sea the same colour of blue as Lily's eyes and the golden sand of the beach was the colour of her hair. He had the window down and the scent of frangipani in the air reminded him of her perfume and, if he closed his eyes, the warm ocean breeze on his face could be mistaken for her soft breath on his skin as she lay curled into his side. Even after two years he could instantly recall how the weight of her head felt on his shoulder as they lay naked in bed, her long hair splayed across his chest, her fingers resting on his thigh.

In London he'd almost been able to ignore the absence of Lily. They hadn't been in the city long enough to establish a history of time spent together there and there hadn't been the constant reminders of her on every corner, but in Sydney everywhere he looked, everywhere he turned there was another memory. The beach, their favourite coffee spot, their local pub and the cinema where they'd seen their first movie together. The past was everywhere but what of the future?

He sighed as the taxi driver dropped him at the house on Moore Street. His house.

He had the keys in his pocket but it didn't feel like his house, or even their house, any more. He felt like a stranger. It was Lily's house now.

He stood on the front step and took several deep breaths to calm his nerves before pressing his finger to the doorbell.

The sound of the doorbell made Lily jump. She'd been on edge ever since she got home. No, ever since Otto had appeared at the hospital. She hadn't been able to work out what he was doing here and why he hadn't told her he was coming back. She hadn't worked out how she *felt* about him being back. She had so many questions but no answers.

She'd fled from the hospital the minute her shift had ended, wanting to put some distance between them, wanting time to clear her head but her thoughts had been going round in never-ending circles.

The doorbell rang a second time and she headed down the hallway. She breathed deeply, trying to calm her nerves, a sixth sense telling her that Otto was standing on the doorstep. She would have liked more time to compose herself but she knew she had to face him at some point.

She turned the handle and despite mentally preparing herself the sight of Otto standing on the step still made her heart race.

'Hello, Lil.'

He leant towards her and Lily panicked. Was he going to kiss her? She wasn't sure but she knew she wasn't ready for that. She was discombobulated enough. She turned her head and his lips grazed her cheek.

He smelt fresh, as if he'd just stepped out of the shower, and she could feel the warmth of his body. She moved back. Her self-control had never been good around him and she needed to keep him at a distance. She'd finally worked up the courage to raise a difficult topic of conversation with him, thinking he was thousands of miles away, and she couldn't drop her guard now.

She could see the confusion in his eyes caused by her avoidance of his kiss but he didn't question her. She'd longed for his attention two years ago, she'd longed for him to acknowledge her pain, their loss, to share the heartache and to comfort her but he'd shut her out. Throwing himself into his work and leaving her to deal with her grief and now the combination of shock and anger made her react without thinking. She hid behind the door, shielding herself from his affection and attention as she ran her eyes over him, taking stock, looking for changes in his appearance that she might have missed in one of their infrequent video calls.

He wore a short-sleeved polo shirt that was snug across his broad chest and exposed his arms. His arms were muscular, well-defined. She'd always loved his arms and they looked as strong as ever. His olive skin looked as if it hadn't seen a lot of sun lately, he was paler than she remembered, but she knew it wouldn't take long for his skin to tan in the Australian summer. He was still lean, she thought, as she looked for differences.

He was thirty-four, four years older than she was and she noticed some grey scattered through his dark hair, not much, but that was something new. It didn't detract from his looks, it was just a sprinkle, just enough to show the passing of time.

But despite the years that had passed he still looked good and there was no denying, in her eyes at least, he was still the most handsome man she'd ever seen.

'What are you doing here?'

'You said you wanted to talk,' he replied. 'Can I come in?'

His head was slightly angled as he watched her, his dark eyes questioning. The street was quiet but she was sure he hadn't come all this way to have a conversation on the front step. She nodded and stepped back.

'I thought you were still in London,' she said as her heart rate finally slowed and began to resemble something close to normal. Something that didn't make her fearful that it was going to leap out of her chest or, alternatively, suddenly give up altogether. 'When did you get back?'

'Yesterday.'

'*Yesterday!* Why didn't you tell me?' Her head wasn't spinning any more even if her mind was and she felt as if she were operating on autopilot as she turned and walked down the narrow passage, past a bedroom to her right until she reached the point where the house widened out, opening into the lounge room, which led to the kitchen. She didn't need to direct Otto, he knew this house better than she did. It had been his house before they'd met. Before they'd got married.

'I meant to. I called you when I landed. Didn't you get my message?'

'Yes. But you didn't say anything about being back. You ambushed me at the hospital.'

'I wanted to surprise you.'

Mission accomplished, she thought as she collapsed onto the couch.

'Shall I take these to the kitchen?' he asked and it was only then she noticed he was holding a bunch of lilies and a bottle of wine.

She felt like bursting into tears. Part of her wanted to fall into his arms, to let him soothe her soul, but he hadn't been good at that. That was one of the reasons she'd left London in the first place. Otto, the man who wanted to fix things, hadn't been able to fix her. She was still fragile. She couldn't deny she was drawn to him, that she still felt a physical attraction, that had never changed, but it was her emotional needs that he hadn't been able to meet.

She took a breath and held her tears in. She couldn't fall apart now. She'd had a plan before he'd rung the doorbell and she couldn't change course now. She had wanted to talk but a cosy catch-up wasn't what she'd had in mind. When she'd initially decided on her plan a face-to-face conversation hadn't even been on her radar. She'd imagined having this conversation over a video call with him in London. Would she be able to remain on track? Focused on the conversation she wanted to have now that he was here in person? She was already finding it unsettling to have him in the same room as her. It made the situation very real and far more personal than having a video call. It wasn't going to be as easy to keep a clear head when she could see him in the flesh. When she could see *all* of him, not just bits. When she could reach out and touch him. When she could smell his aftershave.

She was shocked and stunned but somehow, she held herself together. She shook her head as she tried to clear her thoughts. 'I wasn't expecting to share a bottle of wine,' she told him. 'I wasn't expecting flowers.'

'I didn't want to turn up empty-handed.'

She couldn't remember the last time he'd bought her flowers. They'd never had the money to spend on little luxuries like fresh flowers. She didn't want to refuse his gifts but she didn't want him bringing her flowers either. In her mind it complicated things and that made her response a bit terser than she intended it to be. 'I wasn't expecting you to turn up here,' she said.

'You said you wanted to talk,' he repeated. 'I assumed you meant in private. This seemed like the best place.'

She suspected the talk he envisaged was rather different from what she had in mind. She wasn't planning on sharing a bottle of wine and reminiscing about their past. Their paths had diverged a long time ago. She had a plan for her future.

'Just let me put these down,' he said, gesturing with the wine and the flowers.

Her heart was racing again and her hands were shaking. She knew that was caused by the adrenalin coursing through her, a result of the slight shock she was experiencing at his appearance, but she couldn't let herself be distracted by his presence. She'd made a list in preparation for the phone call she had imagined them having but she now felt woefully unprepared. She'd never imagined this conversation was going to be easy but it now felt almost impossible.

She needed to remember her plan. She was going to move ahead with her life.

Seeing her siblings find love had been the sign that made her realise she'd been living a lonely existence. She had put her personal life on hold for two years, she couldn't blame Otto, and she didn't, not completely, this was on both of them. It was time to reset her personal goals and work towards them.

Having Otto back in Australia wasn't enough. Not unless they were on the same path and she suspected Otto's path was now a long way from hers. Two years of heading in different directions would put them miles apart. In two years they hadn't spoken about what happened next and she couldn't rely on Otto to give her what she wanted. If he wanted a family he would have told her before now. If he didn't want a family yet then she needed a divorce.

It was time to let go of Otto. Of the dream of raising a family with him, of having his children. It was a dream she'd had from their very first date. She knew that was why she'd held on as long as she had. And it was a dream that was hard to let go of. Even harder now that he was back in her space. But she'd have to relinquish it if she wanted a chance of realising the dream at all. She needed someone to have her back and she wasn't sure if she could trust Otto to be there for her.

She needed to find someone who wanted to walk beside her into her future. Someone who was happy to share her path.

It didn't matter that he was there in person, she told herself as he came back, empty-handed, from the kitchen. That didn't change anything. He might only be back temporarily. He might have come back to ask *her* for a divorce. She needed to stay firm. She needed to stay resolute.

'I wanted to talk to you about getting a divorce,' she blurted out the minute he stepped back through the doorway. She didn't know how to break it to him gently. She worried that his presence would distract her and make her waver. She was worried he could change her mind. She had to stay strong. She'd made her decision.

Otto's blood ran cold and he could have sworn his heart skipped a beat, if not several. He'd been unsure of the reaction he was going to get when he arrived at Lily's door and he wasn't sure what he expected the conversation to entail but he knew for certain he hadn't expected divorce to be the first topic of discussion she would raise.

Her words punched him in the face. He was stunned. Completely blindsided.

He knew they had things to sort out. After two years apart he wasn't foolish enough to think they could act as if nothing had happened and they hadn't left each other in a good place so of course they had work to do, but divorce? He'd made a commitment to Lily for life when they exchanged wedding vows. She had too. You didn't walk away from that at the drop of a hat. She could argue that two years wasn't the drop of a hat but there were a lot of factors at play and divorce was not an option. Not in his mind.

He put his hand on the back of the couch to steady himself, relieved he'd put the wine in the kitchen—there was a good chance he would have dropped it on the floor after hearing Lily's bombshell.

He was struggling to breathe and little black spots danced in the corners of his vision. He took a moment to force air into his lungs, to combat the feeling of utter terror that swamped him. He hadn't tried to stop her when she'd left him—maybe he should have but he knew she'd needed her family around her. He hadn't been able to fix her, he hadn't been able to give her what she needed, all he'd been able to do was let her go. But he'd had no intention of letting her go permanently. He'd assumed she'd come back to him. Maybe that had been a mistake. But he wasn't going to give in without a fight now. There had to be something he could do.

He forced his feet to move and somehow made it around to the front of the couch. He sank onto the cushions, facing Lily across the low coffee table. 'You want a divorce?'

She nodded.

'When did you decide this?'

She shrugged.

'What does that mean?' he asked, unable to decipher her gesture.

'I've been thinking about it for a while. Wondering what we're doing. What the point is of being married any more.' She wouldn't meet his eyes and he knew there was something else going on. Something she wasn't telling him.

'What do you mean what's the point? Marriage is a commitment. We made a commitment. To each other. You don't just give up on that and you don't get to make a unilateral decision.' He knew they had unresolved issues but he hadn't, in a million years, expected those issues to bring them to this. She was his wife. He loved her and he wasn't going to give her up quietly. There had to be something he could do. He had to fix this.

'I'm not,' she argued. 'I think we should talk about it, that was why I called and left you a message, but I think a divorce makes sense.'

He couldn't disagree more. 'Sense? How on earth does it make sense?'

She was frowning. A little crease appeared between her blue eyes. 'This can't come as a complete surprise. We haven't lived together for two years.'

'Because you left me!'

'You didn't try to stop me.'

When Lily had told him she wanted to go home, to leave London and return to Australia he hadn't argued. He was frantically busy with his work and study and Lily was spending a lot of time on her own. He figured she needed a break and he was happy for her to go, he didn't know how else he could help her. When he'd said goodbye, he'd done so assuming that she would return to London at some point. But he hadn't counted on a global pandemic. He knew she could have returned despite what was happening in the world—it wouldn't have been easy but it was far from impossible. She had a work visa. She could have come back at some point in the past two years. But she hadn't.

And he hadn't been in a position to go after her. Until now.

'I thought it was what you wanted,' he said. 'I thought you wanted a trip home.'

'It wasn't what I wanted. But I couldn't stay. I needed to come home.'

She was right, he hadn't tried to stop her from leaving but he wasn't going to take all the blame. He had been committed to his fellowship but he'd never wavered in his commitment to his marriage. But what about to Lily herself? Had he given her the attention she needed? He knew he hadn't made her needs a priority after she'd left, he'd focused on his work and had figured he'd make it up to her later. But the months had passed and they'd remained apart. He realised now that they'd each been waiting for the other one to come back and it seemed Lily had grown tired of waiting.

Well, he was here now. And there was one thing he was certain of. 'I didn't come back from the other side of the world to get a divorce.'

'I didn't know you were coming back.'

He'd been foolish not to tell her that he was coming home but he'd been frantic trying to speed up the process of moving and starting his new position. He'd decided to surprise her even though he hadn't been a hundred per cent certain of the reception he'd get but this was completely unexpected. She'd checkmated him with a surprise of her own.

'Can I ask you why you've decided now that you want a divorce? Why not six months ago? A year ago?' There could only be one reason, he suddenly realised as his stomach turned. 'Have you met someone else?'

Lily was shaking her head. 'No.'

Thank God, he thought, as a small semblance of hope returned. From the first moment he'd laid eyes on Lily he'd known he wanted to get to know her and from their first date he'd known he wanted to marry her. That meant spending the rest of his life with her but of the five years they'd been married they'd spent two of them apart. Was that too long? Or was this one case when time would heal all wounds? He didn't know the answer to that but he would find out.

He had no idea.

His biggest regret was that he hadn't known how to help Lily. He liked to fix things but he hadn't been able to fix her. He'd been at a loss. Her physical injuries had healed but the emotional wounds had been harder to treat. He knew his actions had compounded her emotional scars and so, to lessen his guilt over the part he had played, he'd let her go.

Now he was nervous, uncertain, and it was an unpleasant feeling. He always looked for the positives in a situation, practising mindfulness, something he'd worked hard on after his mother had died and he'd learned that even on a bad day there was usually something good to be found. He didn't mind a challenge but he felt as if he was three steps behind Lily and that put him at a disadvantage. But he refused to give up. He wouldn't give in. He knew he would fight for her but if she wasn't prepared to surrender he wasn't sure what he could do.

'Does the fact that I'm back change things?' His motto had always been not to worry about things he couldn't change but he wanted to change her mind.

'I don't know.'

She was fiddling with her wedding ring, spinning it on her finger. The movement caught his eye and buoyed his sprits. She hadn't removed her rings, surely that was a good sign?

Otto reached out and ran his thumb over the gold band on her finger. 'You're still wearing your wedding ring,' he said.

Lily's heart leapt and her breath caught in her throat. She resisted the urge to close her eyes, to curl her fingers around his hand, to pull him close.

The touch of his thumb on her skin sent her pulse skyrocketing. She knew there was no truth in the folklore that a vein connected her ring finger directly to her heart but it certainly felt like it to her. She hadn't counted on feeling so connected to him still and her physical reaction to him took her by surprise. Emotionally she was still fragile, still desperate to hear him acknowledge her pain, but there was no denying there remained a connection between them. A connection wasn't quite broken yet.

Which was one reason she still wore her

wedding ring. It was a part of her. A part of her dreams, and taking off her rings was going to be the last step, the point of no return, and a step she wasn't prepared to take until they were divorced. Was she still holding out hope that they could fix things? Was she scared? Frightened?

She'd never wanted to remove her rings and, in a way, keeping them on her finger kept her safe. Despite being separated from Otto by oceans and time she hadn't been at all interested in other men and if she looked married it discouraged men from asking her out. She suspected that didn't bode well for finding a partner in the future but she'd take it one step at a time. And the first step was getting a divorce. She knew that while she remained legally married to Otto she wouldn't be able to move on. It wouldn't feel right.

'We're still married,' she said as she pulled her hand free and covered her rings, knowing she would have to remove them if she got divorced. That thought scared her a little. She'd have to join the dating scene. She hadn't really thought that through. In her head she had gone from married to Otto to having babies but she hadn't thought about *how* she was going to meet someone to have babies with. Ever since she'd met Otto she'd never looked at another man. Her attraction to him had been immediate and complete and every cell in her body still remembered him. Just like the day they first met.

She had been a final year med student. He was a registrar. Lily had noticed him the moment she'd stepped into the ICU. He was standing beside the specialist, she no longer remembered who the specialist was or what the patient's diagnosis had been and she didn't think she knew at the time either—Otto had captured her attention and that was it.

She had noticed him immediately and their eyes had locked but she hadn't been able to maintain eye contact. She'd looked away, forced herself to focus on the patient but she hadn't heard a word that anyone else in the ward round had said. She'd felt Otto's eyes on her the entire time.

He was tall, dark and handsome and exuded confidence but it was so much more than that. He didn't pretend that he wasn't looking at her but his attention hadn't made her uncomfortable. She was used to attention, she was tall, blonde, athletic and she knew she was considered pretty, but she wasn't confident and she didn't court attention. She usually tried to make herself less noticeable. But she was drawn to Otto. She had a sense that they were supposed to meet, that their paths were destined to cross. She would normally dismiss that feeling as ridiculous hippy nonsense born out of her childhood growing up in a commune, but the sense that their souls were speaking to each other, as stupid as it sounded, was too strong to ignore. She didn't *want* to ignore it and at the end of the ward round she found herself concocting a question and directing it to Otto, making sure he had to answer her. He'd offered to go over some case notes with her, they'd chatted and laughed, he'd invited her for a drink after work and they'd been together ever since.

He was funny, cute, confident and self-assured. He knew what he wanted and she found that attractive. Growing up, she'd been surrounded by drifters. No one on the commune ever seemed to have firm plans or any desire to achieve anything other than to get to the next day. They took everything one day at a time but Lily wasn't wired that way and she often felt as if she was the only one with goals, as if she was the odd one out.

She had one goal in mind. To get out of Byron Bay.

She'd studied hard with that goal in sight and when she'd been accepted into medical school at the age of eighteen she'd left Byron Bay and headed to university in Sydney. She hadn't looked back.

She'd felt a calling to medicine. When Lily was fifteen, her eight-year-old sister, Willow, had died after contracting mumps. Willow had been Daisy's identical twin, the youngest of the five Carlson siblings, and if Lily's parents had believed in childhood vaccinations, then Willow, in all likelihood, would still be with them today.

Daisy had also contracted mumps and had lost her hearing as a result of the viral infection. She was now profoundly deaf but Willow's death had impacted on all of the siblings in different ways and it had solidified Lily's ambition to become a doctor. She *wanted* to save lives. If it was in her power she would prevent any other family, any other siblings, from experiencing what she and her brother and sisters went through.

Getting into university, studying medicine, had become her focus. She'd had no plan for her life past finishing university. That had seemed a monumental goal at the time and it was all she could manage. She'd had one plan, one goal, and she figured she'd work out what to do next once she'd achieved that first step.

But Otto had known exactly what he wanted. In life. In his career. And he knew when he met Lily that she was the one for him. That knowledge had bolstered her confidence. She'd been buoyed by his adoration, his conviction that they were meant to be together. She'd been swept along by his belief that anything was possible as long as they were together.

And together they had a plan.

Until the plan went awry and she had fled home, alone.

But now Otto was back. Without warning, without reason. She needed to know what he was thinking. She needed some answers.

'Why are you here?' she asked. 'In Sydney.'

'It was time to come home. I'd finished my fellowship and I had a job offer here.'

There was no mention of her, his wife.

He hadn't come back for her, she realised. For them.

There was no them. Not any more.

'I'm taking Leo Atwill's job,' he continued. 'You know he's retiring?'

Lily nodded; it had happened suddenly but she knew Leo was retiring for health reasons. But Otto's announcement felt like a knife through her already bleeding heart. 'You came back here because of the job? Not for me?' She hated that she was asking but she couldn't stop herself.

'Of course, you were part of it.'

'Bu you didn't even discuss it with me?' How important was she if he didn't even bother to mention his plans?

'It all happened in a hurry,' Otto continued. 'There was a lot to organise but it seemed serendipitous that a job came up at Bondi General. I thought it would be nice to work together. You don't look like you agree?' he said, reading the uncertainty in Lily's expression.

She hadn't ever worked with Otto. She'd been a medical student, then an intern, then a registrar but they'd never worked together and she was kidding herself if she thought she was going to be able to work with him regularly without getting caught up in memories. Not even memories. Her reaction to his unexpected touch had nothing to do with memories and everything to do with chemistry. Neither her head nor her heart nor her hormones had forgotten him. How was she going to manage?

She would have to find a way.

And quickly. Otherwise, she would have to look for another job and she didn't want to leave Bondi General. She loved her work. She loved the fact she was close to home, close to the beach, that she worked with good friends not to mention her sisters. She wouldn't let Otto's arrival push her out but she knew it was unlikely that he would move. He'd just arrived.

She'd have to find a solution.

'Working together might make things awkward when we get divorced,' she said.

'I don't want a divorce,' he countered.

'We haven't lived together for two years. The courts would grant me a divorce on the grounds that we have been separated for more than twelve months.'

'Have you looked into it already?'

He sounded unhappy. 'No,' she said. 'But I know from other friends that's how it works.'

'But we're not officially separated,' he argued. He closed his eyes and tipped his head back, lifting his hands and running them through his hair. He let out a heavy sigh and opened his eyes, looking directly at Lily. 'You have to see this has come out of the blue for me. You've taken me completely by surprise.'

'I felt the same when you turned up at work today.'

'I didn't intend to spring my return on you like that. I wanted to see you before I started work, I planned to. I wanted us to have a private conversation but obviously it didn't turn out that way and I'm sorry. Look,' he implored, 'I realise we're not going to be able to sort this out tonight but do you think you could hold off making any decisions for now?'

'What are you suggesting?'

'Don't do anything. Sit tight. Don't file for divorce until we've had a chance to have a proper conversation. I'm jet-lagged and a bit shell-shocked to be honest. I need some time.'

'How much time?' She frowned.

'Can you give me three months?'

'Three months!' She'd thought he might say a few days but months! 'What will another three months achieve?'

'It will give us time to see how we feel. To see if we can fix things.'

Otto *always* thought he could fix things.

'Not everything can be fixed,' she retorted. 'Some things are too broken.' *She* felt broken. 'I don't know if I can give you months.'

'Why on earth not? When we got married you promised me a lifetime. Surely you can give me another three months.'

Lily took a deep breath as she tried to get her emotions under control. It was true, she'd made promises that she'd had every intention of keeping but things hadn't turned out quite like she'd expected. 'That was before,' she said.

'Before what?' he asked, as if he didn't know. As if he couldn't guess.

She could feel the old wounds beginning to gape again. Thoughts she'd worked so hard to suppress. Did she have to spell it out for him? 'Before we lost our baby.'

'Lily, if I could go back in time and change that, I would. You know I would.'

'Do I know that?' she asked. 'I have no idea what you'd do any more. Not after that. You didn't want children back then. You never wanted that baby.'

'That's not true.'

'Why would you go back and change what happened? I want a family,' she continued without giving him a chance to argue his point. 'That's why I need a divorce. I can't have a family on my own. I need to start again.'

'You don't need to start again. I'm right here.'

Did she dare believe they could make their marriage work? She knew they had things to resolve but if he was willing to start a family would she be prepared to work on their relationship? Could it be fixed? She wasn't sure but if he was ready to have a family she knew she'd be willing to negotiate her position. It wasn't to say they didn't have other issues to sort out, she still didn't know if she could trust him to support her if things went wrong, but what if he was ready to have a family?

'Do you want children?' she asked. 'Right now?'

He hesitated and she knew the answer.

'We agreed to wait until you were thirty-two,' he said. 'Until we'd established our careers.'

'I've changed my mind.' She realised she'd moved the goalposts but only after they'd been accidentally moved two years ago. That event had been enough to change her mindset.

'Why?'

She'd put her dreams aside for the past two years but now they were back in full force. 'I have a hole in my heart and the only way I can fill it is with a family of my own.'

'Lily, please, can't you give us a chance? Can't you give *me* one more chance?'

'I don't know.' Something was missing in her life and she needed to fix it. It was up to her.

All her life, responsibilities had fallen to her. As the eldest sibling she'd taken on the responsibility of looking after her brother and sisters. She'd never had anyone look out for her. She'd always relied on herself. When she'd met Otto she'd thought finally there was someone who would take care of her but he had let her down too. It was up to her to determine her future. 'I need to fix this,' she said.

'Won't you let me help? There must be something I can do? Tell me. Is there any-thing? What about counselling? What if we tried that?'

'What difference would that make?'

'I don't know,' Otto admitted. 'But I'm not just going to give up. Please, Lil, don't throw our marriage away. Three months and some counselling, that's all I'm asking for. Then, if you still want a divorce, I'll give you one.'

Lily knew she shouldn't give in. She was terrified that Otto would break her heart all over again but it wasn't as easy as she thought it would be to give him up. Not while he was sitting in front of her pleading for another chance. Not when she could see his face, hear his voice and reach out and touch him.

Now that the moment was here she was reluctant to give it all away. To give him away. Despite everything that had happened she knew she still loved him. Maybe, just maybe, if he still loved her too, she could convince him that adding children to their lives was the next step they should be taking.

She nodded. She knew she was risking everything but she also knew her heart would break no matter what she did. Did she want her heart broken now or in three months' time?

She closed her eyes. She didn't want to see the pain in Otto's dark eyes, she knew it was a reflection of her own. She didn't want her heart broken now, which meant she had only one option—she'd give Otto what he wanted. 'OK. Three months,' she agreed, crossing her fingers that the potential reward of a family of her own was worth the risk of heartbreak.

'And counselling?'

'I'll think about it,' she replied, buying herself a little time.

She didn't want to discuss her marriage

with a stranger. She didn't want to discuss her failings as a wife because she knew, no matter how much blame she laid at Otto's feet, some of it had to lie at hers as well.

Was she prepared to open herself up to that?

CHAPTER THREE

L<small>ILY WAS ALONE AGAIN</small>.

Otto had left, he'd gone back to his hotel. She felt conflicted about him staying in a hotel. This was his house after all, perhaps she should offer to move out? He should be able to live in his own house. But she knew she couldn't stay there with him.

She was finding it hard to keep her thoughts moving in an orderly fashion. Normally she was focused, able to compartmentalise, but Otto's arrival had her confused. Her mind was muddled and she found herself jumping between thoughts. Her head was telling her one thing but when she saw him, when he smiled at her or touched her hand, her heart told her something else altogether.

No, not her heart. Just her hormones. They'd get used to him being around soon enough, she thought as she sliced some lemon and added it to a jug of water, which she carried out to the deck, placing it on the table, keeping busy as she waited for her sisters. After Otto had left, the house had felt way too empty so she'd messaged her siblings and invited them over. Jet was busy but Poppy and Daisy were on their way. She needed their company—she was worried that if she was alone she might be tempted to call Otto and ask him to come back. It was much better to call her siblings while her mind was in turmoil.

Poppy had offered to pick up takeaway from Lao Lao's kitchen, Jet's fiancée's family restaurant, and Lily had happily agreed. As the eldest sibling she'd always taken on the role of looking after her younger brother and sisters and it was nice to have someone look after her for a change.

'So, I'm guessing you're about to tell us that Otto is back?' Poppy said as she helped herself to another dumpling from a container.

Poppy didn't meet her eye but Lily didn't miss the glance she shared with Daisy and she realised her news wasn't going to be news at all. 'You knew that?' she asked, looking at Daisy, making sure she could read her lips, knowing Poppy would be able to hear her question while Daisy's hearing impairment would make that impossible.

'Ajay told me he'd met him at work,' Daisy said.

'He knew who he was?' Lily realised she'd been foolish to think she could keep her relationship to Otto a secret. The hospital grapevine was constantly working in overtime and with most of Lily's family connected to the hospital in some way her marital situation was bound to be discovered sooner or later.

'He knew your husband is a doctor named Otto...' Daisy said, leaving her comment to trail off and leaving Lily wondering why until Poppy filled in the gap.

'He might have heard Otto was coming back.'

'How?' Lily frowned. *She* hadn't even known. Daisy's fiancé, Ajay, worked in the emergency department with Lily—he would be no more privy to who was being hired than she was.

'I have a confession to make,' Poppy added. 'Ryder and I invited him to our wedding.'

'What? Why?'

'He's family. I didn't want to exclude him.'

'Our parents are family too but you're not inviting them.' Lily knew Ryder had suggested a couple of times to Poppy that she should invite her parents, worried that she might have regrets later, but Poppy remained resolute and her parents remained uninvited.

'I wanted Otto to be there. I thought you'd be pleased to see him.'

'He told me he came back because he was offered a position at Bondi General.' Lily was confused. 'He hasn't mentioned your wedding.'

'He didn't come back because of our wedding. When I invited him he said he was coming home anyway. He'd already accepted the job at Bondi General, our wedding just gave him a deadline.'

'Why didn't you tell me you'd invited him?'

'I assumed he would.'

'Well, he didn't.'

'I didn't realise he hadn't.'

'You're not pleased he's back?' Daisy signed.

'Maybe a year ago I would have been,' Lily replied, using her hands to communicate. All the Carlson siblings had learnt to sign after Daisy had lost her hearing as a child. Daisy often preferred to use sign language, particularly in a group situation, as she found it hard to follow multiple conversations if she had to lip read.

'What does that mean?' Daisy hands fired back another question.

'I feel a bit unravelled by it all, to be honest,' she admitted.

A year ago her biological clock hadn't been ticking as loudly as it was now. Now it threatened to drown out every sensible thought in her head any time she found her mind wandering. A year ago she thought she could have looked at Otto without noticing the passing of time, without feeling the absence of children—not just the baby they'd lost but all the future children she wanted. She was running out of time but she didn't know if she was going to get what she needed from Otto. She had no idea if he was going to be prepared to meet her timeline. Was she wasting precious weeks by agreeing to counselling? By agreeing to give him those three months?

'I don't know what to think. What to do. What to say. I wasn't expecting him and I'm not prepared for this.' She realised that was one of the biggest factors contributing to her sense of upheaval. She hated feeling unprepared. All her life she'd committed time and energy to preparing for things—from tests, exams, job interviews and holidays, right through to Sydney and then London—she never went in blind. Her unconventional, chaotic and crazy childhood had taught her that she coped best if she knew what was coming, if she felt ready. Otto should have known that about her and she found herself a little irritated that he'd put her on the spot by arriving unannounced. She wasn't prepared in any way for his return.

'How is he?' Daisy asked, as concerned as always for everyone's feelings.

Lily shrugged. 'Fine.' Otto had an unwavering sense of optimism. Things had pretty much always worked out for him so why wouldn't he have a positive disposition? Even after her announcement she could tell he felt that this was just a glitch, a problem to solve, something to be fixed, and she knew he thought he'd be able to fix it. She wasn't so sure. But her sisters didn't know about the grenade she'd lobbed at Otto the moment he'd arrived home. She'd have to tell them.

'Maybe you just need some time to adjust to having him back,' Poppy suggested.

'Maybe...but I'd just made some big decisions and now he's back and it's messing with my plans.'

'What sort of big decisions?'

'I told him I want a divorce.'

'What? Why?'

'You can't divorce him. He's your person.'
Poppy and Daisy objected simultaneously.

'But what if he's not my person?'

'What do you mean?' Daisy asked.

'I know you think there's a person for everyone but there has to be more than one,' Lily argued. Plenty of people found love a second time around. Daisy's fiancé, Ajay, was a prime example. He'd been married before, happily married until tragedy struck, but he'd fallen in love with Daisy as well. But Lily wasn't going to give specific examples. She didn't want to remind Daisy of Ajay's past. She knew it as well as Lily did. 'And what if I chose the wrong person to start with?'

'No.' Daisy was shaking her head. 'I've seen you with Otto, we all have and yes, I know that some people are lucky enough to find love more than once but all of us fall hard and fast. I've decided that it's a Carlson trait. Look at Jet and Mei, Poppy and Ryder. They fell hard and fast and even with other relationships in between that love never died. Nothing else they found could compare to how things felt when they were with the one. I look at you and Otto and I see the same thing.'

Lily wasn't so sure. She used to think she and Otto were destined for each other but things had changed.

But what if Daisy was right? What if Otto was the only one for her? What if she was about to throw away her future? What if she never found happiness with someone else?

But she'd never know if she didn't try. 'We've been apart for almost two years,' Lily said. 'I can't waste any more time.'

'This is your marriage! You're not wasting time.'

Daisy might think Otto and Lily were meant to be but Daisy had always had a rose-coloured view of love. And just because Daisy thought the Carlsons were the type to give their hearts away once and only once didn't mean that Lily couldn't be the exception to the rule.

She and Otto had married quickly, they'd had a whirlwind courtship and then spent almost half of their married life apart. She had nothing to measure their relationship against. How was she to know if he was the right one for her, the only one for her?

How had they let themselves get to this point?

* * *

'Can you tell me what brought you here today?'

Lily perched rigidly on the edge of the sofa in the therapist's office, feeling as if she was getting ready to bolt for the door at any moment.

Poppy's fiancé, Ryder, had recently started work as a psychologist. He worked with at risk teenagers but had passed on a recommendation for a marriage counsellor. Lily had agreed to counselling, knowing she would recommend the same to her siblings or friends and knowing she owed Otto that much at least. She just hoped it wasn't a waste of time. She didn't think counselling would fix their problems but perhaps it would give them closure on their relationship.

She looked around the room, trying to calm her nerves. The space was decorated in neutral tones, with pot plants to soften the space and sheer curtains at the open window. The counsellor had positioned a small three-seater couch opposite her armchair and there was a second armchair to the right of the couch. It looked like a lounge room and was obviously decorated with the aim of relaxing its occupants but despite that Lily was on edge and she was aware of Otto's tension as well. But while she was stiff and uptight his unease made him restless. He'd chosen to sit on the couch with her, ignoring the single armchair. Was that habit, for show or did he really want to sit beside her? She didn't know.

She returned her attention to the therapist. What had Helen asked? Why were they here?

Lily had known they'd be asked that question but she found herself suddenly unprepared. She was nervous, anxious, tongue-tied. It reminded her of the feeling she'd experienced before oral exams in medical school. What if she didn't know the answer? What if she got one wrong and the lecturer thought she didn't know her topic?

She thought about her answer now. Was it wrong to open with 'I want a divorce'?

Was that still what she wanted? She had agreed to give him three months. Perhaps it would sound better if she said she wanted a fresh start. But was that too ambiguous? Did she want a fresh start with Otto or with someone new?

She sighed. A fresh start with Otto wasn't possible. Not after everything that had happened. It wasn't easier to start again but it would be less painful. She couldn't look at Otto without remembering what she'd lost.

'Otto? Lily? I need to know why you're here today,' Helen repeated.

Lily flinched.

She was here because Otto had asked her to come. Because she'd told him she wanted a divorce. She needed to be honest. She owed it to herself and to Otto.

Otto and Helen were both looking at her, waiting for her to speak. Why did she have to go first?

'I want a divorce,' she said. She'd wanted to sound so certain, so sure of herself, but her mouth was dry and her voice was barely above a whisper. Her future without Otto had been so much easier to imagine while Otto was on the other side of the world. It was *a lot* harder when he was sitting beside her.

'And I don't,' Otto stated.

Lily couldn't help but notice how determined he sounded even though there was nothing he could do to prevent a divorce, nothing except try to change her mind.

'I am used to seeing couples who have differing points of view, it goes with my job, and I appreciate you've both taken time to come to see me today,' Helen replied. 'So that I can understand your situation, can you tell me what you are hoping to achieve through counselling?

'Maybe it would be easier for you if I explain how I see my role,' she continued when neither Lily nor Otto were forthcoming with any more details. 'My role is to help you work through what your issues are. What your needs are. To help you work out if these are things that you can work on, if these are things you *want* to work on. It might be behaviours that need to be modified, it might be expectations. And that will be the case for both of you. I hear you already have differing points of view. This is your opportunity to work out if you are prepared to consider working together on your marriage or if it's time to step away. We will not be apportioning blame. Marriage is a partnership and you have to work together if you want it to be successful.

'I will give you things to think about,' Helen said, 'things to talk about, but I cannot give you the answers. I can't tell you what to do nor can I make the decisions for you. It is up to the two of you to determine where you go from here. If I can start with you, Lily. You said you want a divorce.' She paused, waiting for Lily's response.

Lily nodded.

'I'm a counsellor, not a divorce lawyer. Why have you chosen to come to counselling?'

'Otto asked me to.'

'Why did you *agree* to come?' Helen rephrased her question.

Coming to counselling was a way to assuage her guilt for her part in all this. She'd blamed Otto but she was the one who had walked away from their marriage. It had been easier to walk away, to try to outrun her sorrow, than to confront their issues and she felt guilty for that.

Staying in London would have meant seeing Otto every day. Being reminded of everything they'd lost. Being reminded that there were still only two of them when there should have been three and that she was partly responsible for that. Running away had meant she could avoid thinking about what had happened, to some degree. Putting some distance between her and Otto had let her forget what had happened, if only for short periods of time. But some respite from her guilt, her sadness, her loss, was better than none at all. Some respite had allowed her to function. Running away had enabled her to avoid admitting to her role in the tragedy.

She was still avoiding it.

And that was why she had agreed to come. It was easier to agree to counselling than it was to apologise for her part in all of this.

Was it also easier to ask for a divorce than to ask for forgiveness? Was it easier to ask for a divorce than to apologise?

It must be.

'If you've already decided you want a divorce, I take it you're not interested in saving your marriage?' Helen asked when Lily gave no response. 'What do you need from me?'

Did she want to save her marriage? She would have said yes two years ago, even one year ago, but now? Now she felt their paths had diverged too much. She wanted babies. He didn't. It was as simple as that. 'I thought maybe you could help us to communicate better with each other.'

'Has that been an issue?'

Lily nodded again. 'We seem to have difficulty discussing the important things. Like divorce. If Otto and I don't agree that a divorce is the best thing for us, then that's a difficult conversation to have. I thought you might be able to help us with that process. I don't want to fight. I don't want to argue. I just want to move forward with my life. I thought counselling might give us closure.'

Lily could feel Otto tensing beside her. She didn't need to be looking at him to be aware of his reaction. Every one of her nerves was still attuned to him. Physically they were connected, it was emotionally where she felt the divide. His physical reactions were always obvious to her but his thoughts were harder to decipher.

'Otto?' Helen asked. 'Why did you choose to have counselling?'

'Definitely not to help us get divorced. The opposite. I hoped it would help us work out a way forward—together.'

'You understand that might not be possible?'

'Yes.'

'Tell me about your situation,' the therapist asked. 'How long have you been married?'

'Almost five years. That has to be worth something, doesn't it, Lil?' Otto looked at her, his brown eyes dark and imploring.

Lily couldn't hold his gaze. She could see his pain, she felt it too, but the pain they shared wasn't lessened by sharing. Seeing him was a reminder of everything they'd lost and she couldn't trust him not to break her heart all over again.

He'd promised to take care of her. To love her always. And she felt he'd abandoned her at the first obstacle. In their marriage vows they'd promised to support each other but when things went wrong it hadn't brought them together, it had torn them apart. She turned back to Helen. 'But Otto has been in London for two years. We've been living apart.'

'That was your decision, Lily,' Otto said.

'Otto,' Helen interrupted. 'Let Lily talk. You will have your turn.'

'He didn't even tell me he was coming back,' Lily continued, ignoring Otto's comment. He was right, she had chosen to leave but he hadn't come after her, he'd chosen to let her go. 'That's just one example of our lack of communication. We used to be able to talk to each other.'

'What changed?'

'Lily stopped talking,' Otto replied as he turned to face her. 'You shut me out. You wouldn't tell me how you were feeling.'

She'd been scared to start talking, scared she'd lose control and wouldn't be able to recover. Scared of where she would end up.

'I was feeling the same way every day, alone with my sadness, alone with my grief, alone with my loss.'

'It was *our* loss, Lily,' Otto stressed, before

telling Helen. 'We lost our baby at twenty-one weeks. That was when things changed.'

Helen was silent for a beat or two before asking, 'Do you want to talk about your loss, Lily?'

Lily shook her head, the irony not lost on her. She wanted to talk to Otto but she wasn't ready to talk to a stranger about their baby even if she was a counsellor. Lily's grief was still too raw to share with anyone else. It was personal. It was between her and Otto.

Lily knew it would be difficult for counselling to help her if she wasn't prepared to unpack some of her emotional baggage but then, she hadn't really expected counselling to help anyway. If she could learn how to find forgiveness, that would be a start.

She was aware that Helen was observing them. It made her nervous. What was she looking for? What did she see?

'You were in London together?'

Lily nodded.

'But you came back alone?'

'Almost two years ago.'

'Why did you do that?'

'I needed things that I couldn't get in London.'

'Like?'

'Comfort. I needed comfort and company.'

'But Otto was there.'

'Physically, yes. But not emotionally. We weren't communicating. I barely knew anyone and after our loss I felt even more alone. Adrift. I needed my siblings and I needed the ocean. This ocean.' She waved one arm in the direction of the Pacific Ocean. She and her siblings had spent their childhoods in the ocean, swimming and surfing. It was where she found calm, it was where her soul was restored. 'I needed to see it. I needed to be in it. And I needed to see the sun, to feel it on my skin. This is my home. I needed to come home.'

'Did you intend to go back?' Helen asked.

'I don't know.' She'd been so intent on leaving she hadn't thought about what came afterwards. About how long she'd stay away. She hadn't really intended not to go back but she hadn't returned either. She'd been in limbo. And she'd stayed there for two years. There were too many painful memories in London.

'You said you and Otto used to be able to talk to each other?'

Lily nodded.

'Do you agree, Otto?' Helen asked.

'Yes.'

'I'm going to give you some homework. Do you remember your first date?'

'Yes,' they answered simultaneously. Lily could feel Otto looking at her but she refused to meet his gaze this time. She didn't want to share that moment. She needed to block out those memories if she wanted to move forwards.

'Where did you go?'

'We went for a drink at a bar near the hospital where we met,' Otto replied.

'Good. I want you to go out together. I want you to talk to each other as if you've just met. Get to know each other again. Listen. Put everything that has happened aside, just for the moment,' Helen added, probably in response to Lily's expression.

'What is the point in that?' Lily asked.

'It's an exercise in listening. I don't want you talking about big things, things that require debate or discussion. I want you to talk about simple things. Practise your listening skills, show an interest in what the other person is saying without having to think of an argument. Without conflict, without agenda. Talk about what you do in your spare time, about your hobbies, the movies you like, your favourite places to visit. Think about all the things you wanted to know about each other when you first met.

'You need to open the lines of communication but you need to choose a neutral topic,' Helen continued. 'Something that isn't associated with your relationship, something that isn't raw and emotional. Something that won't lead you to judge each other's feelings. You can work your way up to those big discussions once you feel that you can trust each other to be honest. Once you know you can listen without judgement. When you can listen without assuming how the other person is feeling. I want you to start over.

'Do you think you can do that, Otto? Lily?'

Lily nodded. She wasn't sure but she was prepared to give it a try. She had never been given a homework task that she hadn't completed and she couldn't agree to counselling and then refuse to commit to the process.

'There's a bar across the road,' Otto said as they left Helen's office. 'Shall we go there?'

'You want to do this now?'

'Why not?'

Lily could think of a million reasons why not, including the fact that she would prefer time to prepare mentally for the homework Helen had set them. She'd prefer time to think about some safe, neutral topics of conversation and to find a safe, neutral venue. A wine bar wasn't what she had in mind. 'You want to go to a bar? This isn't a date. It's an exercise.'

'That doesn't mean we can't enjoy ourselves, that we can't have fun. You do remember how to have fun, don't you?'

She was too embarrassed to admit that maybe she didn't. Otto was always the one who brought the fun to their relationship. She was much more serious. Her life before she met Otto hadn't been a lot of fun and life without Otto *definitely* hadn't been fun. But she wasn't going to tell him that.

'Come on, let me buy you a drink.'

He grinned at her and held out his hand and she could feel her resistance folding. She'd have to work on strengthening her resolve if she hoped to execute her plan. She couldn't afford to let Otto back into her life. There was too much at stake.

But she had agreed to the homework so she crossed the road but ignored his outstretched hand. Not that Otto seemed to mind. She could tell by his expression that he was taking her acquiescence as a victory to him. She'd let him have this one but the battle was far from over.

There was a small courtyard at the back of

the bar and Otto found them a table for two under the vines. It was a lovely evening to sit outdoors, warm and still. He passed her a drinks list. 'What can I get you?' he asked.

'I'll have a gin and tonic, thanks.'

'Would you like anything to eat?'

She shook her head. Having something to eat would take longer and she would find it more difficult to escape. One drink would be enough.

'Where shall we start?' Otto asked as he returned from the bar with their drinks.

'I don't know, this feels so pointless.'

'What does?'

'Having to sit here and make small talk,' she said. 'I already know everything about you.'

'It's homework, Lil. Do you want to go back to Helen and tell her you didn't do it?'

She'd always been studious. She knew she wouldn't. And Otto knew that too. 'No.'

'We've got two years of catching up to do. I don't really know what you've been up to although Jet tells me he is a father, which makes you an auntie.'

'You've spoken to Jet?'

'We've stayed in touch.'

Lily knew Otto had spoken to Poppy but she didn't realise he 'kept in touch' with any of her siblings on a regular basis and hearing it was Jet was doubly surprising. Lily sometimes wondered if Jet would keep in touch with his own sisters if they didn't make an effort but Otto had always got along well with her family. His willingness to embrace her siblings was one of the many things she'd found attractive about him and that didn't seem to have changed. She wondered what else about him hadn't changed. There were some things she wanted to stay the same and others she needed to know had evolved.

'So, I have a niece.'

She nodded. 'I guess you do.'

'And An Na is what…seven?'

'Yes. She's amazing and Daisy is going to be a stepmum to a two-year-old, Niki.'

'I've met Ajay. He seems like a good bloke.'

'He is. Daisy is madly in love.'

'So all three of your siblings are settling down.'

Lily nodded. 'It's been a whirlwind five months.' And it had reignited her desire for a family of her own and had put her on the path to asking Otto for a divorce. 'It's ironic, isn't it?'

'What is?'

'I'm the one who desperately wants kids

and Jet and Daisy will both have a family before me. Poppy probably will too.'

'You've got a family. You've got me.'

Lily shook her head. 'You know what I mean. I want kids.'

'I do too.'

'But not right now.'

'No.'

'Why not?'

'I want to get my career established first. We've talked about this.'

'Are you prepared for it to cost us our marriage?'

'I'm hoping it won't come to that,' he replied.

'It will unless one of us changes our minds. Otherwise nothing will be resolved.'

'Let's see what happens,' he said.

She knew he was expecting her to change her mind. He should know better.

The timely arrival of a waitress at their table broke the thread of the conversation. She delivered some small share plates—flatbread and dips and salt and pepper calamari with golden fries. Lily pinched a chip from the bowl. If she had her mouth full she wouldn't be expected to talk.

'I thought you weren't eating?' Otto teased as he pushed the bowl closer to her.

'They smell so good,' she said.

'I ordered extra… I knew you'd want some. You always did prefer to eat off my plate.'

That was true. No matter what she ordered when they ate out she always ended up preferring whatever Otto had ordered. He'd always been happy to share and there were plenty of times where he'd even swapped orders with her. She'd forgotten how generous he was in some ways.

'What do your parents think of becoming grandparents?' Otto asked as she sampled the calamari.

Her parents were far from typical and if Lily hade ever entertained a notion of them changing their ways she was yet to see any evidence of it. Even the arrival of grandchildren wasn't enough to bring out their nurturing side.

'They haven't met An Na yet.'

'No?'

'Dad had a cerebral aneurysm about the same time that we found out about An Na.'

'You didn't tell me.'

Lily thought he could add that to the long list of things she'd never told him. She didn't have a close relationship with her parents—growing up on a commune hadn't fostered close ties and she disagreed with a lot of their beliefs. Her strained relationship with them meant they rarely entered into her conversations, with Otto or anyone else. She shrugged. 'He's recovering well but they haven't been down to Sydney. They don't seem in any hurry to meet An Na or Ajay's son, Niki.'

'They're still living on the commune?'

'Yes.'

'Have you seen your dad since his aneurysm?'

'The four of us did go up to Brisbane while he was in hospital but that was a few months ago. It was an interesting visit. Dad was quite forthcoming about their history, it was a bit of a revelation actually, and he apologised for some aspects of our childhood but while I appreciate the fact that he acknowledged their actions impacted us it didn't really atone for their behaviour. It doesn't excuse some of the things they did. Living on the commune was an easy way to opt out of responsibility and that is fine if you've only got yourself to think about but they had five children. Even if they were living in denial in the early years you'd think after Willow died they might think about the consequences of their choices and decisions and how that affected us. I'm not convinced they did their best in raising us and apologising now doesn't change that. They haven't changed either, they are still each other's priority. The four of us are a long way down their list and I don't think the arrival of grandchildren is going to change them. I don't think they'll necessarily want any involvement with grandchildren or that my siblings will want them involved.'

'Will they be at Poppy's wedding?'

'No.' They hadn't been at Lily and Otto's either.

'You know Poppy and Ryder have invited me. Is that OK with you?'

'It is.' Lily wasn't going to tell Poppy who she could and couldn't invite. 'We're working together anyway. I can't avoid you.'

'Do you want to?'

The honest answer was no but she knew it would make her life a lot easier if she did keep her distance. She'd be able to keep a clearer head for a start.

As he waited for her answer Otto reached across the table. 'Hold still,' he said as he stretched out one hand. 'You've got aioli on your face.'

He brushed his thumb over her cheek, running it across her skin from the corner of her mouth. His hand was warm, his touch gentle and it made her breath catch in her throat, made her forget the question.

It was so long since anyone had touched her like that—gently, with familiarity—and it felt so intimate. Her body still knew him even if her mind was trying to forget. It was the same when he'd run his thumb over her wedding ring. She'd missed that sensation. Would she find that connection with some-one else or was Daisy right? Was Otto her person?

No. If he didn't want kids he wasn't her person. He couldn't be.

Lily stood up. It was time to go. The things she liked about Otto hadn't changed. He could still make her laugh. He could still make her pulse race. He still made her feel alive but she knew they still had hurdles to get over. What she didn't know was if they were hurdles she had the energy to jump or if they were barriers she couldn't control. Were they hurdles Otto had to take down or ones she had to learn to live with?

That was a dilemma for another day but she knew she didn't have infinite days to answer the questions. She had a biological clock and it was ticking. And she knew it would get louder as Poppy and Daisy started families of their own. She was thirty years old. She was torn and confused and she wasn't sure she could continue like this for three months. She'd go mad.

CHAPTER FOUR

'INCOMING AMBULANCE,' JULIE announced to
the ED. 'Jet ski accident. Teenager with suspected spinal injuries.'

'I'll take it,' Lily responded. 'Who's the
trauma surgeon on call?' she asked, knowing it was better to forewarn the specialist,
knowing in this instance it was unlikely they
wouldn't be required.

'Otto. I'll page him now.'

Of course, it would be Otto, Lily thought.
She hadn't seen him since the re-enactment
of their first date two days ago because she'd
been on days off, but it was becoming obvious that it was going to be impossible to
avoid him at work.

She took a deep breath to calm her heart
rate. There was always a spike of her pulse
whenever an ambulance was expected as
adrenalin kicked in when an emergency was
announced. It mattered not that she felt con-

fident in her skills—that fight-or-flight response was triggered every time and flight was not an option. But she knew her heart rate had escalated more than normal and she knew that, along with the flight response preparing her to deal with the emergency, there was an element of flight response as a reaction to knowing Otto was on his way.

She changed her gown, replacing the dirty one with a fresh one, along with fresh gloves. She could hear the approaching siren and she hurried to the ambulance bay, leaving the ties of her gown undone. Someone would do them up for her outside.

Otto followed her out of the hospital. She saw him in her peripheral vision as he strode out to the ambulance bay, his inherent confidence evident, looking as though he'd been working at Bondi General for years, not days.

She listened as he greeted everyone by name. She knew he would have made a conscious effort to get to know the names of colleagues. He was good at making friends. His father was a defence force doctor and Otto had moved frequently as a child and he'd become adept at making friends easily out of necessity, but he was a social person by nature too. He enjoyed company, the bigger and louder the crowd, the better. Lily was happier in a small group of close friends or family.

'Hey, Lil.' He greeted her last. She frowned at his intimate abbreviation of her name. She'd asked him to keep their relationship a secret for now. Her colleagues knew she had a husband but she didn't need them to know it was Otto. Not yet, not while they were sorting out their relationship. There was nothing to tie them together, neither of them had worked at Bondi General before they'd moved to London and she practised under her maiden name so keeping their marital status private was going to save them from being the subject of any gossip. As a school-girl she'd been gossiped about on plenty of occasions because of her family's living ar-rangements on the commune and she'd learnt to avoid giving people any ammunition.

'Otto.' She kept her response brief. De-spite not wanting to advertise their relation-ship she was annoyed that he'd greeted her last. As if she wasn't important.

She was still conflicted. Irritated on one hand, drawn to him on the other. She couldn't pretend that the sight of him didn't set her heart racing.

She turned her back slightly. If she avoided

looking at him she'd give her pulse a chance to slow down.

'Do you want me to tie your gown?' he asked, obviously seeing the loose ties as she'd turned away from him.

His arrival had distracted her and she'd forgotten to ask someone to do it for her. Before she could answer, before she could say no, he had stepped behind her. She jumped as his fingers brushed the nape of her neck. She had to force herself not to close her eyes as long-forgotten memories of his warm hands on her skin threatened to overpower her. Her body remembered him and she could feel herself wanting to sway towards him. She took a deep breath, clenched her fists and tensed the muscles in her legs as she fought to stay still.

Did his fingers linger a little longer than necessary on her shoulders? Or were her senses heightened? She wondered how she was going to extricate herself from the situation when she felt his hands drop away.

'All done,' he said as the ambulance pulled into the bay, allowing her to take a step forward, putting some distance between them and enabling her to recover her equilibrium.

She breathed out and let her shoulders

relax as her future sister-in-law climbed out of the driver's seat.

Otto greeted Mei as if they were old friends and Lily wondered when they'd met. It must have been in the past couple of days. He hadn't said anything about meeting Mei when they'd gone for their 'date'. Why hadn't Jet and Mei included her when they caught up with Otto?

But she knew why. Because of the bomb-shell she'd dropped on Otto.

That didn't stop her from feeling irritated. She had never been one whose emotional responses had easily seesawed but since Otto had reappeared in her life her emotions seemed to be in a constant state of flux.

Jet was *her* brother, which made Mei *her* family. Why did Otto get to spend time with them?

The answer was simple—Otto and Jet were friends, and she couldn't do anything about that.

But what would that mean for her future? It was just another thing she hadn't considered.

When she'd decided she wanted a divorce Otto had been overseas. Having him back in Bondi was a scenario she hadn't thought about and it was obvious there was going to be a flow-on effect—to her at least. But she'd have to deal with that later, she thought as she switched her mind to their patient as the back door of the ambulance was opened and the stretcher was unlocked.

'Patient is a nineteen-year-old girl with head and suspected spinal injuries,' Mei told them as the stretcher was unloaded from the vehicle. Lily could see the girl had been intubated and immobilised to protect her spine from movement. 'She was a passenger on a jet ski with a group of friends,' Mei continued. 'There were multiple watercraft, she came off and was hit by the jet ski that was travelling behind. She was possibly hit in the head. Her friends dragged her from the water before lifeguards reached them. GCS of seven.'

That wasn't good. Three was the lowest possible score and a Glasgow Coma Scale score of between three and eight indicated severe traumatic brain injury.

'Oxygen sats were eighty-nine per cent but climbing with treatment.' Mei continued to relay the patient's vitals. 'Pupils were equal and reactive.'

'Let's get her inside,' Otto instructed. 'Do you know if she's had any alcohol?' he asked as he helped Mei and Alex push the stretcher into the ED.

'I'm not certain,' Mei replied.

Lily knew alcohol could adversely affect the outcome in patients with a TBI. 'Do you know her name?' she asked.

'Chelsea.'

'All right,' Otto directed. 'Let's transfer her on the count of three.'

They slid her carefully onto a hospital bed, five of them working together, and Otto barely stopped his assessment. 'I need blood tests, including alcohol levels, a full blood count and I want her ABGs monitored,' he said as he connected the patient to a ventilator.

She observed and listened to Otto as he communicated with the staff and his non-responsive patient. He was confident and assured, directing the staff clearly, concisely and politely. He worked without ego and was obviously good at his job and Lily found his professional demeanour attractive. But she didn't *want* to find new things about him attractive. It was hard enough that her body betrayed her every time he was nearby, she didn't need her mind confusing her too.

'Lily, can you repeat the GCS, please?' Otto asked as he connected a monitor to

Chelsea's ventilator to measure her exhaled carbon dioxide levels.

Lily ran through the tests for verbal performance, motor responses and eye opening. Chelsea had no verbal response, but that was to be expected given that she was on a ventilator. She did withdraw from pain when Lily forcefully squeezed her trapezium muscle but her eyes remained closed in response to the painful stimuli.

'GCS is five.' That wasn't good news. Mei had earlier reported a score of seven.

Otto looked up. Lily could see he was worried but there was no sign of panic. He picked up a torch and checked Chelsea's pupils. 'Left pupil five millimetres, nonreactive. Right, two millimetres and sluggish,' he recounted. They all knew that the information indicated raised intercranial pressure meaning that Chelsea most likely had bleeding in or around her brain.

'Theatre?' Lily asked and, when Otto nodded, she lifted the phone and repeated the same procedure as on Otto's first day in the hospital, only this time she made sure she wasn't the one accompanying Otto in the lift to Theatres. Drama seemed to be following Otto, she didn't plan on doing the same.

* * *

'Chelsea didn't make it.'

Judging by the expression on Julie's face, Lily expected her to be the bearer of bad news but this was worse than she feared. Her first thought was that it was a tragic outcome for Chelsea's family, an afternoon of fun on the water had ended in tragedy with one life lost and plenty of other lives would be changed for ever as a direct consequence, but then her mind went straight to Otto, as it had been doing all afternoon.

Chelsea had certainly been in a critical condition when she'd been brought to hospital but sometimes the odds were in the patient's favour and sometimes they weren't. The news that she hadn't survived shocked Lily but her sympathy lay with Otto.

How would he be feeling?

She knew he would be hurting. She knew it hit him hard when he lost a patient and she knew he hated having to be the bearer of bad news to a grieving family but she was conflicted. He'd never admitted to struggling emotionally when it had been the two of them suffering a loss. When they'd lost their own baby, he'd kept a stiff upper lip, he'd never showed any outward signs of despair or distress. She'd never been able to tell if his stoic countenance had been his way of coping or if the loss had not felt real to him. Had it been an intangible concept? She had been the one who had felt the baby move and grow inside her. She felt as if she'd known, almost from the moment of conception, that she was pregnant. She'd felt different. But she understood how foreign it might feel to a father, to Otto. That until he could hold the baby in his arms it might not feel real. But she had no idea about his mindset really. He'd never shared his thoughts or feelings with her about that time of their life.

But even if he wouldn't verbalise his feelings, she knew Chelsea's death would have affected him. What she didn't know was what, if anything, she should do next. Should she leave him to it? Should she seek him out? Was it any of her business any more?

She hated to think of him having no one to turn to if he needed a shoulder. A friendly face. Some support. Could she offer that to him?

She was the one who knew him best.

He had no one else.

She called past his office at the end of her shift but it was empty. One of the cardio-thoracic administration staff members told her that he'd left for the day. In the past he would have sought her out after a day like this, he would have wanted her company. Knowing he hadn't looked for her felt strange, upsetting, but she knew she couldn't have it both ways, not after she'd raised the topic of a divorce. She had no right to be hurt. He'd be hurting more than her.

She could have left it there, she could have gone home, but having decided to find him she now felt compelled to do so. If she found him and he didn't want her company he could tell her as much. She knew where he would have gone. He would need to let off steam and, like her, swimming cleared his head. He would be at the beach. What she didn't know was which one, but she'd start at Bondi. It was the closest.

She walked down to the beach, covering the few hundred metres in no time. She stopped near the lifeguard tower and leant on the railing that separated the parked cars from the beach. The elevation gave her a good view of the kilometre-long stretch of sand curving from the ocean pool in the south to the headland in the north. But it wasn't the sand she had her eye on. She swept her gaze over the ocean. It was after six but the summer heat was still intense and the beach was still busy but the real swimmers were few and far between and it didn't take her long to spot Otto. He was out past the breaking waves, swimming parallel to the shore and heading south towards the lifeguard tower.

The afternoon sun was warm on her back as she watched him swim. His strokes were even, smooth, hypnotic. She didn't mean to wait for him but she was still standing by the railing when he turned towards the beach. She could have left then but her feet weren't moving and she was still there when he came out of the water.

His chest was smooth and pale. He hadn't had time yet to catch any sun. His swimming shorts clung to his thighs. He might be pale but he was in good shape. Superb shape, she thought as she took in the seminaked sight of him.

He hadn't seen her and she watched as he walked up the sand towards her. He looked good. Better than she remembered. Had she forgotten or had she stopped paying attention?

He'd left his towel in front of the tower and he bent down to retrieve it, throwing it over his head and rubbing his hair dry. She remembered how he never bothered to dry his skin after a swim and sometimes even after a shower. She felt a blush steal across her cheeks as she recalled how, after showering, he'd stand at the mirror, naked, while he shaved or wander around the house naked while his skin dried. He would let the water evaporate from his body but he always dried his hair. It was sticking up now, stiff with salt.

He threw his towel over his shoulder and looked up. He smiled as their eyes met and she waited to see what he would do next.

He made his way across the sand and jogged up the stairs beside the lifeguard tower, coming to a stop beside her. 'Are you looking for me?'

She nodded. 'I wanted to check how you were.'

'You heard about Chelsea?'

'Yes. It sounded pretty awful.'

Otto wondered what it meant that Lily had come to find him, that she was checking in with him. Could he take it as a good sign? He wasn't sure. He didn't want to get his hopes up or make assumptions. He'd keep the conversation on a professional level.

He nodded. 'It was. She had severe trauma with a massive amount of cerebral haemorrhaging and I suspect spinal cord damage as well.' They'd tried their best but sometimes there was nothing that could be done. They were doctors, not magicians. 'If she'd survived, she'd have been severely disabled but that doesn't make it any easier for the family. The news is still devastating for them.'

It had been devastating for him as well. He knew he'd found it particularly hard today because he was already feeling unsettled. Lily's bombshell had disturbed him and he didn't need another wave to swamp his already leaky boat. He felt as if he was just holding on as it was. But none of those feelings were things he wanted to talk about. Talking about it wouldn't change what had happened and he'd learnt not to spend his energy worrying about things he couldn't change.

He'd come to the sea to clear his head. The ocean was calming and he'd missed it while he'd been in London. Swimming laps in a pool wasn't the same and it had been good to be back in the sea. It was good to see Lily too but he didn't need her help. The swim had given him time to reset and he wasn't going to dwell on what had happened. Chelsea's death didn't sit well with him, of course it didn't, he hated losing patients, but he knew that sometimes it was inevitable. He'd done his best and that eased his conscience and he had to put the events of the day behind him. Tomorrow was another day. Tomorrow he'd be back at work doing it all over again, hopefully with better outcomes.

The lifeguards were packing up the beach, taking down the flags, bringing in their boards, putting the warning signs away. It was time to go. 'I left my phone and keys in the tower with Jet. I'd better grab them before they lock up for the night.'

Lily looked at him quizzically before she nodded. 'You sure you're OK?'

'Yeah. I'm OK.'

He wasn't. But not for the reasons Lily thought. He hated losing patients but he'd learnt to accept that he couldn't save everyone. He wasn't infallible, he wasn't perfect. He could accept that. It was one reason why he'd chosen trauma as his speciality. He didn't have time to build relationships with patients, which meant it hurt less if things went badly. As a trauma surgeon he could deliver bad news and then move on. He could provide fleeting comfort to a family in their time of need without providing counsel. He didn't need to become invested in their heartache, he didn't need to share their experience of loss and grief, he didn't need their grief to stir up reminders of his own. He didn't want to remember how he'd felt as a teenager after losing his mother.

It didn't mean that losing a life wasn't difficult but as long as he had done his best he could accept the inevitable and ultimately he knew he saved more lives than he lost. He'd learnt to accept the losses that came with the job, but he couldn't accept losing Lily. He couldn't accept that their marriage was over. He wasn't prepared to accept that divorce was inevitable.

Coming back hadn't turned out as he'd expected and he still didn't know how to fix things but in his mind their marriage was salvageable and he wasn't giving up until he'd figured out how to save it. So, even though his world was unsettled, even though *he* was unsettled, he told her what she wanted to hear. 'I'm OK.'

Lily looked as if she was about to close the gap between them. As if she was about to reach for him. His spirits lifted and he almost stepped towards her but the look on her face stopped him. There was kindness in her expression but no love and he knew she was offering the comfort of a friend. He could see compassion in her eyes but also pity. He didn't want her pity. He didn't want to show any weakness. That was something that had been instilled in him and his brothers by his father. He admitted it wasn't necessarily healthy but it was a habit that was hard to break.

The lifeguards were pulling down the shutters on the tower windows, putting the tower to bed for the night. Otto knew they'd be locking the door next. He didn't need Lily's pity. He didn't want it. It was time to go. He stepped away and said, 'I need to go, I'll see you at work.'

'I've got the day off tomorrow,' Lily replied. 'I'll see you at our next counselling session.'

Frustration and longing, fear and disappointment churned in his gut as he watched her walk away from him. He didn't want her pity but he wanted her. He wanted to go after her. To tell her he was sorry. To ask her again for another chance but he knew his words would be wasted. He knew it was actions she needed from him. He'd have to figure that out. And figure it out quickly, he realised as he headed into the tower.

'A few of us are going to grab a meal at the pub. You're welcome to join us,' his brother-in-law extended the invitation as he handed him his phone.

'Thanks, but I'll give it a miss. I've had a tough day at work.' He didn't want to go out for beers with the boys. He'd wanted to go home with Lily. He wanted to curl up beside her, to hold her in his arms. To bury his face in her hair, to feel her curves under his hands. He knew that would ease the stress of the day.

'You sure? A beer might be just what you need.'

But Otto knew he wouldn't be good company. The swim hadn't really helped. Not in the way he needed but a beer wasn't the answer. 'Maybe another time.'

Should he arrange to catch up with Jet independently? he wondered. Should he ask his advice? He and Jet were friends but Jet was still Lily's brother. Who would he prioritise? Would he take Lily's side? Would he think Lily's request for a divorce was warranted?

Otto decided he wasn't ready to hear Jet's opinion. Not yet.

Admitting he couldn't solve his own problems didn't come easily. Admitting he was wrong was even harder.

'How are you both?' Helen asked as Lily and Otto sat down for their second counselling session.

As Otto sat beside Lily again on the small couch she thought she should have chosen the single chair, but she couldn't move now. That would look like an obvious slight and there was no need for that. Instead she picked up a loose cushion and held it on her lap as a mini shield. Against what she wasn't quite sure.

'How did your exercise go?' Helen continued once they were settled, if not comfortable. 'Did you manage to complete it?'

Lily nodded.

'And how did you feel afterwards?'

Lily didn't reply. She'd felt a tumult of things. She'd felt sad. She felt as if she'd wasted time. She felt as if she'd made poor decisions even when she knew she hadn't. She wasn't sorry she'd married Otto but she was sorry she was getting divorced. Not because she thought it wasn't the right thing to do but because she had never wanted it to come to this. But she couldn't see any way around it. Not yet.

She'd agreed to counselling but she now thought it was a mistake. Unless Otto agreed to start a family there was no way of saving their marriage. She wasn't sure if she could sit through counselling, waiting for him to make a decision. She wasn't sure she could bear it. She wasn't sure if her heart could take it. Spending time with him, raising her hopes, only to have them dashed if he didn't change his mind. It would break her. Again.

'I don't feel like it achieved anything.' Otto spoke up. 'We had a perfectly civilised drink and conversation but at the end of the day nothing has changed. I think it's safe to say Lily hasn't changed her mind and neither have I. We're still diametrically opposed.'

'The point of the exercise wasn't to solve your differences,' Helen reinforced. 'It was to practise talking and listening. Did you do that?'

'Yes,' Otto replied. 'Finding general topics of conversation wasn't difficult.'

They'd spent far longer together than Lily had anticipated and she wondered if Helen would be surprised to hear how easily the conversation had flowed. If it would surprise her to hear how much Lily had enjoyed Otto's company. She didn't think anything they'd said or done yet was unexpected and she didn't want to be just like any of the hundreds of couples Helen might have counselled over the years. Lily wanted to be different. More complicated. More challenging. More important. She wasn't sure what that said about her. She'd always been competitive and obviously nothing had changed—even if she was getting divorced she wanted to be doing it well. Would that shock Helen?

'What did you talk about?'

'Nothing important,' Otto said.

Lily frowned in disagreement and Otto's comment prompted her to speak out. 'We talked a little about work but mostly we talked about our families. Both of those things are important. To me, anyway.'

'Are you both close to your families?'

'I'm close to all my siblings,' Lily replied. 'I see one or more of them every day.' Her relationship with her siblings brought her immense joy. Her relationship with her parents, on the other hand, was much more complicated. But Helen didn't question her about her parents. Lily didn't imagine that it had gone unnoticed that she hadn't mentioned them and she found herself wondering what significance Helen put on that.

'And, Otto? How about you?' Helen had paused before addressing Otto and Lily wondered if that had been deliberate. If she was waiting to see if Lily added any more information.

'You want to know about my family? How is this important?' Unlike Lily's relationship with her siblings, Otto's life was completely independent from his family.

'How you were raised has a big impact on a lot of things,' Helen replied. 'It shapes you. Your family and how you were brought up will influence how you see the world and will influence your expectations of relationships.'

'My family is scattered all over the world so seeing them recently has been difficult.'

'Would you usually see them frequently?'

Otto shook his head. 'I have two older brothers but we're not in regular contact. We get along when we're together but in our day-to-day lives there's no need for contact. I speak to my father occasionally.'

Lily could hear the tension in Otto's voice and she knew he was unconvinced that trawling through his childhood was necessary. Even though she knew, they both knew, the research said differently she was inclined to agree with him, but she knew that was only because she was as reluctant to talk about her childhood as he was. She was happy to talk about her siblings but there was a lot to unpack in her history. While the spotlight was on Otto she was OK, but she knew Helen would turn it on her at some stage.

'And your mother?' Helen asked Otto.

Otto shook his head. 'My mother died in a car accident when I was thirteen. Three months later my brothers and I were in boarding school.'

Lily could hear the pain in Otto's voice. She knew he'd never forgiven his father for sending them away. For not acknowledging their grief. Otto used humour to mask his pain but Lily suspected that could only work for so long. Helen had been on the money—family had a lot to answer for.

'And how often did you go home?'

'That would depend.'

'On what?'

'On where home was. My father is a doctor in the defence force, we moved every three years. Sometimes it was easy to go home, sometimes it was easier not to.'

'And before you went to boarding school. Did your mother work?'

'That also depended on where we were living. She did some volunteer work but she gave up her career to support Dad in his and to raise us. Dad was the head of the household but no one argued with Mum either. They presented a united front to us and there was no dissension in the ranks. Our upbringing wasn't strict, as such, but we definitely had structure. Rules were set and expected to be followed. As the youngest of three brothers, I guess I had a tendency to push the envelope but my brothers and I mostly had each other's backs. We got into mischief but we learned to get ourselves out of it. I don't know if that was Dad's influence or if it was by necessity to save Mum's sanity. Dealing with three boys couldn't have been easy.'

'But your mother had the primary responsibility of raising you?'

'Yes. I guess they had fairly traditional parenting roles. Until she was killed.'

'Do you have similar expectations about marriage and family dynamics? About who would support whom?'

Otto paused and looked at Lily. 'I don't know that I ever thought about it specifically. I guess I imagined we'd support each other.'

'So when you got pregnant had you talked about what the future would look like? How you would raise the baby?'

'No,' Otto admitted. 'The pregnancy wasn't planned.'

'Were you planning on having a family at some point?'

Otto nodded.

'But you hadn't discussed the details? Who would raise the children? Did you assume it would be like your family? Did you expect Lily to stay at home?'

'I didn't plan on Lily giving up her career.'

'Were you planning on giving up yours?'

'No. That was a conversation for another day. Maybe we'd get help.'

'From whom? Your family? Lily's?'

Otto shook his head. 'No. Our parents couldn't be counted on.'

Listening to Otto answer Helen's questions, Lily realised again how much they'd both assumed things would work out. For someone who liked a plan she couldn't believe how naïve she'd been. Yes, their pregnancy was unexpected but she couldn't believe that at no point had they talked about the logistics of raising a family and what that would mean. It had all been dreams and hopes. Nothing concrete, nothing tangible.

'And when you moved to London, was that for your work or Lily's?'

'We went for my work. But Lily was happy to move.'

'How did you broach that topic? Was it a fait accompli that Lily would go too? Did you have to put your career on hold, Lily?'

'No. I had a job at the same hospital.' Otto was right. She had been happy to go. She had seen it as an adventure, their first real adventure together and she'd wanted to support him. But unfortunately, things hadn't turned out as she wished.

'And how did you find the move?'

'Harder than Otto did if I'm being honest.'

'In what way?'

'Otto was used to moving and having to start over. He moved house every three years and changed schools often whereas I'd only moved once before, when I came to Sydney for university at the age of eighteen. He's more outgoing than me and good at making friends.' Otto had learned to use humour to break the ice and make friends. He was funny and people liked to be around him. He was a good foil for Lily, who had a tendency to take life very seriously.

'I'm not as socially confident,' she added. And she wasn't, by nature, a risk-taker. Otto was always eager to try new things, he was much more spontaneous than she was and she knew that she relied on him to make her push herself. To make her test her boundaries. 'And I missed my siblings. We were close growing up, we still are, so being on the other side of the world from them was tough.' Poppy was only twenty-two months younger than Lily and Jet was sandwiched in between. They'd been inseparable growing up and she'd missed them more than she'd anticipated, especially after she lost the baby.

'Where did you grow up?'

'In Byron Bay. My childhood was probably the polar opposite of Otto's,' she said as she saw Otto smiling. They both knew their families were like chalk and cheese. 'I grew up on a commune.' Lily took satisfaction in seeing that, finally, something she'd said surprised Helen and Helen's expression made Lily more forthcoming with information than she had intended. 'My childhood was chaotic and unconventional. Structure and order were non-existent. We had virtually no supervision. No boundaries. No rules. Now I crave order, structure, routine.' She did not like surprises.

'Your parents didn't adopt traditional parenting styles?'

'Not at all. I virtually raised my siblings. My parents weren't interested in that.'

'How many siblings?'

'Four.' She still counted Daisy's twin, Willow, even though she'd been gone for fifteen years, lost to a preventable infectious disease.

'And you're the eldest?'

'By eleven months.'

'Are your parents still married?'

'My parents are together but they never married.'

'Being married isn't important to them?'

'It never seemed to matter. My father is the single most important thing in my mother's life. He always came first for her. Before any of us children. If she had to choose between him and us she would choose him. Every time.'

'And how do you feel about that?'

She felt a lot of things. Hurt. Upset. Angry. But they weren't feelings she wanted to share. Once again, she could see the irony of her reaction. She was in counselling, she was supposed to open herself up, she was supposed to expose herself, reveal her thoughts and feelings in an effort to communicate better but some things were too painful. 'It made me determined to ensure that my children will know they are special, wanted, important and loved,' she said, censoring her reply but speaking to Otto as much as she was answering Helen.

'And how do you feel about marriage? How important is it to you?'

'It's very important.' She'd only intended to get married once but wasn't that what everyone thought?

'You said you've been living apart for two

years but you have only just brought up the topic of divorce. Why is that?' Helen asked. 'What was the trigger? If marriage is important there must be something more important to prompt this decision?'

'My marriage was important but having children of my own is more important. It was looking like I couldn't have both.'

'We had planned to wait until you were thirty-two. You're only thirty,' Otto interrupted. 'We have time.'

'We might have had time but we'd also have to be in the same place. You were in London, I was in Sydney, things between us were strained, I didn't know where we were headed.'

After the assault Lily had learned to block all thoughts of having babies from her mind. She couldn't face the idea of something going wrong again but seeing her siblings with children of their own and spending time with Niki and An Na had reawakened her desire. Her biological clock was ticking and she needed to satisfy it. If Otto wasn't coming back she needed to look at her options. 'I need to find someone who wants what I want. I can't do this alone.'

'You don't have to be alone, I'm right here. We can try again.'

Lily tried to explain. 'I know we had planned to start a family when we got back from London but when I got pregnant unexpectedly it felt like the right time for me. And then that was taken away.' She was speaking to Otto now. She'd forgotten that Helen was in the room. 'I realise I'm changing the goalposts but seeing my siblings settling down, seeing Jet and Daisy with children has reignited that need in me to have children of my own and time is ticking. My biological clock is ticking.'

'Lily, I promise you, we can fix this. I can fix this.'

'Why do you think everything can be fixed?'

'Because usually things can. Together we can work this out. It's not easier to end our marriage.'

'I didn't say it was easier. Just that it might be better.'

CHAPTER FIVE

'LILY, PLEASE DON'T throw our marriage away yet.'

She remembered what Daisy had said about the Carlson siblings having one true love and it was tempting to let Otto persuade her to hold on to that ideal. She knew not everyone was lucky enough to find love once, let alone twice, but Lily was still hurting. She felt as if she'd failed. At marriage. At being a wife. At being an expectant mother. She'd wanted Otto to protect her as he'd promised but she hadn't protected their baby.

Lily knew she hadn't caused the placental abruption that had ultimately resulted in the loss of her baby but she'd replayed the events of the assault thousands of times and she knew she should have reacted differently. If she hadn't put up a fight, if she'd just let the man take her bag, the outcome could have been different. It was a fact that was hard to come to terms with, almost impossible to accept. She had failed her own child.

She shook her head. She and Otto were two trains at the same station but on parallel lines and she really had no idea how to get them onto the same track. 'Too much time has passed. Too many things have been left unsaid.'

'This is your chance to say those things,' Helen told them. 'But carefully, mindfully. In small snippets.'

'I'm struggling with putting my thoughts and feelings into words,' Lily said. 'I find it hard and Otto's not great at asking questions.'

'Is that true, Otto?'

'Probably. If someone needs something from me I expect them to tell me, otherwise I guess I assume everything is fine.'

'In that case I have your next assignment in mind, then. I want you both to write a letter to each other.'

'About what?'

'Your feelings. The hurt. The slights. The things you are finding difficult to verbalise.'

'Why?' Lily asked.

'How is this going to help?' Otto asked.

'It will give you both time to process your thoughts. It should help you to clarify what your issues are. To work out where and why things started to go wrong.'

'Where do we start?'

'What was the turning point?' Helen said. 'The point where your paths began to diverge?'

'When I got pregnant,' Lily said.

'When we lost the baby,' Otto replied.

Lily was amazed. They couldn't even agree on that! She'd just outlined her thoughts as to when things began to go wrong. Hadn't Otto been listening or did he really see things so differently from her? If that was the case what hope did they have of reconciling?

'The pregnancy upset things for us,' Lily said. 'That was no one's fault—' she apportioned blame for other things but not for the pregnancy '—but I feel like that was when we started having different expectations about where we were headed.'

'All right,' Helen said, 'start there.'

'And then what? We swap the letters? Give them to each other to read?'

'No.' Helen shook her head. 'You read the letters to each other.'

'Read it out loud?'

'Yes. You told me your goal for therapy was to improve your communication skills. I know you could each read the letters in private but I want you to talk about things. Writing down your feelings will help you to own them, to understand them, and then you should find it easier to verbalise them to each other. I would suggest that when you read your letters to each other you give yourself time to process your responses. Don't feel you have to discuss what the other person has written, unless you want to. Once you've written the letters it then becomes an exercise in listening to each other. That's just as important as talking. I'll leave you with that homework and see you at the same time next week.'

'Are we able to push that session out by a week?' Lily asked as they stood up. 'My sister is getting married next weekend and I have a lot going on with that.'

'Of course,' Helen replied. 'The timing of these sessions is completely up to the two of you.'

'We might need to push it out even further,' Otto said. 'I'm away at a conference the following week.'

'You're going to the conference in the Hunter Valley?' Lily asked as they left Helen's office. There was an Emergency Medicine conference taking place just after Poppy's wedding. Lily was registered to attend but she hadn't given it much thought as yet. Her brain space was occupied by too many other things—mostly Otto.

'Yes. Last-minute change. I'm taking Leo's place. He's decided he's not well enough.'

'He was a keynote speaker. Have you got something to talk about?'

Otto nodded. 'I'm working on it. I can present Leo's session but there's also some pretty cool new technology that I want to mention. Some new technology that can connect to your phone and record a heart tracing.'

'You're serious?'

'Yep. It's pretty interesting. Not something we'd use in the hospital but it might be something to have in more comprehensive first-aid kits.'

'I'll make sure to attend your session, then.'

'You're going to the conference?'

'Yes.' She nodded. 'The hospital is sending Ajay and me.'

'Bondi General ED.' Lily picked up the phone at the triage desk and her stomach dropped as she listened to the ambulance dispatcher as he relayed details about the in-coming patients.

'Julie! Ajay! Two incoming ambulances,' she called out as she hung up the phone. 'MVA vs pedestrians.'

'Pedestrians *plural*?' Ajay asked.

Lily nodded. 'Elderly driver. Reports say she hit two pedestrians, an adult and a child.'

'Any other details?'

'No.'

'OK, three patients coming our way. We don't have any patients rating one or two at the moment so I'll free up some hands,' Julie said as she began marshalling staff.

'You take the first ambulance, Lily, and I'll wait to see what we're dealing with,' Ajay said as they headed for the ambulance bay. As the senior ED doctor Ajay got to make that call.

The first ambulance swung into the drive-way and Lily could see Poppy at the wheel.

She switched off the engine and jumped out, giving an update as she moved quickly to open the rear doors. 'I've got two patients on board. A mother and her six-year-old son,' she said as she pulled the door open.

Lily could see a patient strapped to the stretcher. An adult. The mother.

Alex, the second paramedic, was sitting

cradling the child, who was wearing a school uniform and had his left arm in a sling.

'I need a wheelchair,' Alex instructed as he climbed out of the ambulance still holding the child. One of the nurses pushed a chair over to him and Alex carefully lowered the boy into the seat. 'This is Bailey,' he said. 'He's being very brave but he's complaining of a sore right arm. Suspected greenstick fracture of his forearm. Nil pain relief.'

Alex's tone suggested that Bailey was not the patient of primary concern, which left the mother. 'Take him inside,' Lily instructed the nurse, 'but stay with him and nil by mouth.' Bailey's assessment could wait for the moment. But as Raina started to push Bailey towards the ED he began to cry and looked back over his shoulder to his mother.

Lily could see the mother lift her head although the movement was made difficult by the cervical collar that had been placed around her neck. She was strapped onto the stretcher otherwise Lily was convinced she would have jumped up and followed her son. 'I need to go with him.' Lily could hear her distress.

'He's fine. The hospital staff are with him,' Poppy reassured her. 'You need to stay as still as possible.'

'Can I call someone for you?' Lily asked. 'Your husband, partner? A grandparent?' Bailey was going to need someone to support him while his mother was being treated.

'Natalie's husband is on his way,' Poppy said as she and Alex pulled the stretcher out of the ambulance. 'Natalie was struck by the car. Witnesses reported the force of impact threw her into the air and she landed on her left side. She is reporting back and pelvic pain. Possible pelvic or abdominal injuries.'

The patient had been put on oxygen and Lily could see an IV canula in her arm but she was surprised that Natalie wasn't clutching the little green whistle that was often given to administer pain relief.

'No pain relief?'

Poppy shook her head. 'She's five and a half months pregnant.'

Lily could feel the colour draining from her face. A pregnant woman with possible abdominal injuries sustained through a traumatic incident. There were myriad possible consequences of this accident but the first one that sprang to Lily's mind was the potential for placental abruption. She was aware that Poppy was watching her, waiting for her reaction.

'Why doesn't Ajay take Natalie?' Poppy

suggested, knowing where Lily's mind would be going. 'The second ambulance is on the way with the driver of the vehicle. You can take the elderly patient.'

Lily knew there was no likelihood of the elderly patient being pregnant but before she could respond she felt a hand on her forearm, a light touch only, and then a familiar voice. 'Lily. It's OK. I'm here. We've got this.' Otto was beside her, speaking at a volume low enough that his voice wouldn't carry to the patient. He'd obviously heard the description of the accident and he too would know where Lily's thoughts had headed.

Otto waited for Lily to look at him, to acknowledge that he was there and together they'd take care of the patient. Lily looked into his dark eyes as he nodded, very slightly, reassuring her that, at least this time, he was beside her, offering his support.

She nodded in reply. She knew she could rely on him in the ED. She never doubted his professional support, he always gave a hundred and ten per cent to his patients and, by association, to his colleagues. It was only personally she felt he'd let her down.

Had she been too harsh? Too critical of him? Was she expecting perfection? No one was perfect, she knew that, least of all her, she thought as she heard Otto address Poppy. 'What do we need to know?'

'Natalie, aged thirty-six, struck by a car and fell, landing on her left side. Complaining of back pain and left hip pain, able to weight bear with discomfort. BP one-forty over ninety. Heart rate ninety-five BPM. Soft tissue swelling and contusions. Twenty-four weeks pregnant. Third pregnancy. No previous complications.'

'Any abdominal or vaginal bleeding?'

'Nothing visible. She's on oxygen as a precaution. Nil pain relief.'

Otto grabbed the end of the stretcher and looked to Lily. 'You good?' His gaze was intense and helped to settle her thoughts and she knew he was deliberately trying to calm her. She knew there were a number of possible scenarios, multiple possible outcomes for Natalie and perhaps she was being fatalistic but, from her experience, her thought process was reasonable. If Otto thought she was being overly dramatic he kept that thought to himself and focused instead on getting her attention back to the job in front of them.

She nodded. Forcing herself to be positive. Forcing herself to concentrate on the here and now. On this patient. There was no time for memories of the past.

'All right.' Otto increased the volume of his voice and spoke to Natalie. 'Let's get you inside, Natalie. Can you tell me what happened?'

'I was dropping my daughter off at childcare and was taking Bailey to school. We'd just come out of the building. There's a pedestrian crossing in the car park, right out the front, and we were walking across when a woman drove straight through it. She didn't stop. I pushed Bailey out of the way—are you sure he's OK? Where is he?' she digressed, obviously more concerned about her son than herself.

'He's OK,' Lily reassured her. 'He's with the nurses, they'll look after him.'

'Do you remember what happened next?' Otto asked, trying to get Natalie to focus. 'Did you hit your head?'

'I don't think so. The car hit me on my right-hand side. I went flying and landed on my left side.'

'And the pain is in your back and left side?'

'Yes.' Natalie's eyes were darting left and right and Lily knew she was looking for Bailey.

'Your husband is on his way to take care

of your son,' Lily reminded her patient. 'I'll let you know when he gets here.'

'Any abdominal pain? Any cramping?' Otto asked as they pushed her into a cubicle and Lily started connecting Natalie to the various monitors.

'No.'

'Have you felt the baby moving since the accident?'

'I'm not sure.' Lily could hear the fear in Natalie's voice but at least she now seemed able to concentrate on Otto's questions. 'My back and hip hurt so much I'm not sure what else I can feel.'

'And the births of your other children, did you have vaginal deliveries or C-sections?'

'Normal deliveries. I'm not in labour. I know what that feels like,' Natalie said, misconstruing Otto's question. 'This pain is different. I can't be in labour,' she said, obviously thinking that Otto was worried she was going to give birth prematurely. 'I'm only twenty-four weeks.'

'I know,' he reassured her. 'I'm just gathering the details.'

'Lily, can you check the foetal heart rate for me, please?' Lily was testing Natalie's motor responses when Otto interrupted her. Natalie had normal limb strength with moderate discomfort on moving her legs but Lily didn't think she had sustained any significant injuries to her extremities. She stopped the assessment to attach a heart-rate monitor around Natalie's abdomen. Her hands shook as she fastened the Velcro strap. She took a deep breath but it did nothing to steady her hands. She was finding the situation distressing and Otto's calming presence wasn't enough to settle her nerves. Or perhaps it *was* helping, perhaps she'd be worse if he weren't there. She finally managed to fasten the strap, pleased that Natalie wasn't in a position to see her hands, but the tremor hadn't escaped Otto's gaze. She saw him watching her.

'All good?' he asked and she knew he was referring not to their patient but to her. She nodded, determined to get through. She had a job to do.

'Kevin.' Otto took her at her word and continued issuing instructions, this time addressing the nurse. 'Can you cross-match blood type?'

'Natalie, I need to feel your uterus.' Otto pressed gently on Natalie's abdomen. Lily could see there wasn't much give, her belly was hard, and Natalie winced. 'Is that hurting you?' Otto asked.

'Yes.'

'Foetal HR one-fifty and irregular.' Lily's voice wobbled as she passed on the information and Natalie looked up at her sharply.

'Is the baby OK?'

'A little distressed,' Otto responded, jumping in to save Lily from having to answer. 'That's to be expected given what you've both been through.'

Natalie's eyes were wide. She looked from Otto, to Kevin before speaking to Lily as the only other female in the room. 'I need to go to the toilet.'

'Kevin, can we have a bed pan, please?' Otto said before Lily could react.

Kevin helped Natalie to remove her underwear. Natalie's movements were laboured, restricted by pain and Lily could see Kevin was trying to avoid causing her any more discomfort as he helped her.

Kevin dropped Natalie's underwear in a stainless-steel bowl instead of leaving them on the bed and Lily could see the pants were stained with fresh blood. Her heart rate skyrocketed but, with shaky hands, she managed to remove the bowl. She made sure she kept the underwear out of Natalie's sight while letting Otto see the blood. She tried to keep her expression neutral, not wanting to increase Natalie's distress, but she could feel her own anxiety escalate. She checked the monitors. Natalie's blood pressure was dropping but her heart rate was still high.

Kevin whisked the bed pan away as Natalie finished with it and Lily looked to Otto. His return look said 'don't jump to conclusions' but she couldn't help it.

'Natalie, you've got some vaginal bleeding. I need to have a quick look at that. Dr Carlson will stay in the room, everyone else can step out for the moment. Is that OK with you?' Otto glanced at Lily when he mentioned her name. Lily knew he was silently checking with her that she could manage, not that she had a choice—she was the only female member of staff in there, she had to stay. Lily forced herself to block all thoughts of the past from her mind, forced herself to focus on Natalie as she tried to avoid jumping to conclusions.

'Is the baby OK?' Natalie repeated.

'I won't know until we have a look.'

Lily noticed that Otto didn't answer Natalie's question directly, instead he deflected and deferred his answer, choosing to turn up the volume on the foetal heart-rate monitor instead. 'Can you hear that?' he asked. 'That's the baby's heartbeat.' Lily hoped the baby's heartbeat stayed nice and clear and strong. She hoped Otto's demonstration didn't go awry.

The exam room cleared and Lily stood beside Natalie's shoulder as Otto examined the patient.

'I want a sonographer and an obstetrician,' Otto told Lily. Lily could hear the concern in Otto's voice and knew he was worried. She knew he was thinking of placental abruption. She was well acquainted with the condition. Better acquainted than one could ever wish to be.

She wasn't sure how much longer she could keep a brave face. She flicked her gaze to Otto, looking for reassurance.

He nodded his head, just a slight movement but it was a confident one that managed to convey, *You're OK. You've got this.* He mouthed, *You're doing well*, knowing she'd be able to lip-read. She'd picked up the habit from Daisy. She wasn't nearly as proficient but she could decipher common words and basic phrases. She breathed out, exhaling audibly, and the tightness in her chest eased.

'Natalie, I want to take you for an ultrasound scan.'

'What for?'

'Just to check the placenta.' It was less

frightening to say that than to say he was worried about the baby and, technically, what Otto was saying was true. If there was placental abruption and if it was severe, there was nothing that could be done to save the foetus.

'Is my husband here yet?'

'Lily, can you go and see if Natalie's husband is here and check on Bailey at the same time? I'll wait with Natalie.'

Lily knew Otto was offering to wait with Natalie for Lily's sake. So that Lily wouldn't need to answer Natalie's questions. She knew he was getting her out of the room deliberately, trying to protect her, to give her a chance to take a breath, to reset. Had he recognised she'd reached her limit? Did he think she was about to go to pieces?

She stepped out and concentrated on breathing. *Don't think about it*, she told herself. *Don't think about London. Don't think about our baby.*

She should be able to cope, she should be able to deal with these patients and these presentations and she was convinced that usually she would manage. She wasn't sure if having Otto there was making the situation better or worse, easier or more difficult. Having him there was keeping her anchored but his presence also stirred up the memories that were never far from the surface of her mind. Seeing Otto in the flesh brought everything back more vividly and the memories had been bombarding her. Two years had passed but the pain was still sharp, raw, acute. It still took her breath away. But it was more than pain. There were so many emotions. Guilt. Regret. Blame. Anger. Confusion. And, since Otto had returned, all those feelings were much closer to the surface of her mind than they had been for a while.

She was finding it difficult having to mix Otto and her memories with her professional life. Too many parts of her life were coinciding, colliding, and she wasn't able to get any relief. Divorcing Otto might fix one problem in that it would give her an opportunity to begin the journey to motherhood again, but she wasn't sure if she could keep working with him. He was a good doctor, an excellent one, and professionally she knew she could manage but would she be able to separate her personal feelings, her emotional side, from her professional side? Would being divorced make it any easier?

She sighed. That was going to be up to her but she suspected it wouldn't help.

Maybe she'd been approaching therapy

the wrong way, she thought as she checked to see if Natalie's husband had arrived—he hadn't—and then went to get an update on Bailey. Maybe instead of opening up the lines of communication she should be looking for closure. Maybe she should be learning how to forgive, forget and move on.

Perhaps forgiveness was the key. She had to forgive Otto for what she saw as his part in their loss, and for what she saw as his failings as a husband, but she had to forgive herself for those same things too. She'd failed as a mother and a wife and she wasn't going to be able to move on without making a conscious decision to put the past behind her.

And Otto was part of her past.

When Lily returned to Natalie's treatment room with news of Bailey, Natalie's husband had arrived and Natalie had had the ultrasound and had been taken to Theatre.

Natalie's husband was going with Bailey for his X-ray and Otto was waiting to speak to Lily. He closed the door and she knew from his expression what he was going to say.

'She's going to lose the baby, isn't she?' Lily asked. Somehow she thought it would be less confronting if she said the words rather than having Otto tell her but the words caught in her throat and came out as a sob, a cry for help.

Otto nodded and opened his arms, offering her a hug, knowing exactly what she needed. Why was it that he knew what she needed now? Why hadn't he been able to give her the comfort she needed two years ago? she thought as she stepped into his embrace. Despite the regret she felt over what had transpired before, she wasn't going to refuse comfort. She needed a hug. She needed human contact after the day she'd had.

'She had a severe placental abruption,' Otto told her as he wrapped his arms around her and held her close.

She leant her head against his chest as memories of years past rushed back. Memories of hours spent lying in his arms, of feeling his warm skin under her hands, his sculpted muscle under her fingers, his breath on her body, his lips on hers. She closed her eyes as she fought to contain tears of regret. Now that she was in his arms she couldn't remember why she'd refused to return to London. Was she about to give away the person she needed? Was she ever going to be able to replace him?

She wound her arms around him as his

embrace tightened. Did he need the comfort, the reassurance, as much as she did?

'Are you going to be OK?' he asked.

No. She didn't think she was but answering truthfully wasn't going to help anyone. What could Otto do about it? She had a job to do. She nodded. Accepted his hug for just a few moments longer as she composed herself before going back to work.

She had no idea how she got through the rest of her shift, it was all a bit of a blur, but she knew she hadn't made any mistakes. If she'd thought she was in danger of making errors she would have left for the day. It was better to be at work, better to stay busy. She knew the memories would be worse if her mind were still.

At the end of her shift she walked home, thinking about Otto. She wondered if it was wise to go home to an empty house, alone with her thoughts, alone with her memories, but what other option did she have?

She didn't need to talk about the day but she did need company. She could see if one of her ED colleagues was free for dinner, or one of her sisters, any of them would provide her with company but she didn't want to have to explain her day. She wanted someone who would understand what she'd been through without needing to hear it and she knew none of them would get it in the same way as Otto did.

She needed Otto but she needed the old Otto. The one she'd had before they'd lost their child. Before they'd stopped communicating.

While she accused Otto of not wanting to hear what she had to say, of not listening to her, she knew she was partly to blame. She'd been distraught but also angry and guilt-ridden and that maelstrom of emotion had made her shut Otto out. He'd rightly accused her of doing that but after they'd lost the baby she'd needed comfort. She hadn't wanted to relive the experience, hadn't wanted to relive the emotions, hadn't wanted to feel guilty but she had wanted to hear Otto say he didn't blame her. She'd resented the fact that he hadn't tried to comfort her verbally or physically, that he seemed happy to exist in silence and in solitude. She knew she couldn't hold him solely responsible for the breakdown of communication in their marriage. Their marriage had ceased to exist as a partnership, they'd become two individuals sharing a house, and they were both to blame.

Lily lay on the couch as the evening settled around her. She kept thinking she should get up and do something but she couldn't think of anything to do. It was too late to go for a swim or a surf and she didn't have the energy anyway. She probably should just go to bed but she knew she'd just lie there staring at the celling, not sleeping. She'd spent the first hour crying but her tears had eventually stopped although she could still feel where the salty tears had dried on her face, leaving streaks on her skin. She was about to get up to wash her face when there was a knock on the front door.

She ignored it.

There was a second knock. And then she heard Otto calling her name.

She got up. She needed a hug, she needed company, and Otto was there, almost as if he knew she needed him.

She opened the door and stepped towards him. It was automatic, a response born out of old habits, and Otto opened his arms and held her close. She shut her eyes and felt herself relax in his embrace. She wasn't going to cry any more but it felt so good to be held.

'Why are you here?' she asked, her voice muffled against his chest.

'Because you're my wife,' he replied as if that was all that mattered. Maybe it was. 'And I was worried about you.'

'I'm OK.'

'You're not,' he said as he released her and stepped back to look more closely at her. 'I know you think I've got zero emotional intelligence when it comes to your feelings, but I know how hard today was for you and I wanted you to know I'm here for you. You say I don't listen or ask how you are. I'm here, doing both. Have you eaten?' he asked.

She hadn't even thought about eating. She shook her head. 'I'm not hungry.'

'You need to eat. You need some carbohydrates, comfort food,' he said as he bent down and picked up some shopping bags that were at his feet.

'What's all that?'

'Ingredients. I'm going to make you spaghetti carbonara.' He wasn't taking no for an answer and Lily realised she was hungry and Otto was a good cook. Otto's Italian mother had been an excellent cook and she'd passed on some of her culinary skills to her sons before she died and Lily had always loved his pasta dishes.

He followed her inside, poured them each a glass of wine and sat her at the kitchen bench while he cooked. He knew his way around the kitchen and he chopped and fried and stirred and sipped his wine while he chatted about things that had happened during his day, avoiding the topic of Natalie, letting Lily add comments when she felt like it, but mostly she was just content to sit quietly and watch him work. She enjoyed sitting listening to the sound of his voice. It was calming and reassuring. It wasn't the subject matter that was relaxing, he could have been reading her the weather forecast, it wouldn't have mattered, but there was something comforting about the domesticity of the two of them together in the kitchen.

Otto fried the guanciale while the spaghetti cooked before draining the water and adding cheese, eggs and a sprinkle of pepper to the guanciale and pasta.

His movements were smooth and measured, almost automatic. He moved around the kitchen in the same way Lily imagined he moved in an operating theatre—calmly and confidently.

'You still enjoy cooking your mum's recipes?' she asked.

'I do. Cooking was something I have really strong memories of doing with Mum. It keeps me connected to her.'

'Can't you see yourself making those same connections with children of your own?' she asked as he placed a bowl of pasta in front of her. She couldn't stop herself from asking the question. She knew she was having difficulty accepting that he didn't want children yet. She'd always been able to imagine him as a father and she couldn't understand how he couldn't see that, how he couldn't want that experience yet.

'Eventually.'

'Eventually?' Was he going to continue to delay until it was too late for her? Why had she agreed to give him these three months if nothing was going to change?

'Let me explain. I know we planned to have a family but, when those plans became a reality, I admit I struggled.'

'Why?' She'd known he hadn't been as excited as she had been about the unplanned pregnancy but he'd never explained why.

'After Mum died I taught myself not to worry about things I couldn't control. It was how I processed her car accident, by accepting there was nothing I could do to change that outcome, and it became a rule for me to live by. The only time I found myself struggling to live by that rule was when you got pregnant. There were so many things I couldn't control, so many ways I could let our child down, but they weren't things I could ignore, they were things that I felt were my responsibility to manage. But I didn't know how I was going to manage and I freaked out. What if I couldn't do it? What if I let you down?'

'We were doing it together. It wasn't just up to you.'

'In my head, you were my responsibility. Our child was my responsibility. Maybe my letter will explain it better.'

'Your letter?'

He nodded as he cleared their plates. 'I think I should read it to you,' he said.

'Now?'

Otto nodded.

'Why now?'

'I know you're sad. I know you're think-ing about London. About our baby. I'm hop-ing that if we can talk about it, it might take some of the pain away.'

'You think talking about it is going to make me feel better?'

'I hope so. I think Helen is right. We do need to talk about what happened. Writing down my thoughts helped me to understand how I was feeling and also helped me to un-derstand how you might have been feeling. I think you need to hear it.'

'You brought it with you?'

'It's on my phone.'

* * *

When Lily didn't object Otto took his phone from his pocket. He hoped he was right. He hoped that if he could explain his thoughts and feelings to Lily it would help her to understand that the issue hadn't been that he didn't care but that he hadn't known how to help her. He was hoping he could help her now.

He'd come past the house without warning, needing to check on her, but unsure of his reception. When she'd opened the door he could see she'd been crying but getting her to open up was proving more and more difficult. Despite the counselling sessions she still kept her cards close to her chest. He thought perhaps if he went first, if he exposed his vulnerabilities, she might be able to do the same.

He poured her a second, smaller glass of wine and began talking.

'The other day, in Helen's office, you said that our problems started when you got pregnant. That surprised me. I didn't think that was the turning point. In my mind it was when we lost the baby. The first thing I had to do when Helen gave us that homework was to work out where to start so I listened to you and went back to the day you told me you were pregnant.'

They hadn't been in London very long, just a few weeks, and they were still finding their feet when Lily had delivered her news. Otto could still remember how shocked he'd been and he knew he hadn't reacted as Lily had hoped.

'We were still both settling into our new routines, new jobs, a new flat. We were working long hours and getting used to the lack of sunshine at the beginning of an English winter. I'm not making excuses, just acknowledging that we had a lot going on. We were already dealing with a lot of changes and I admit, when you showed me the pregnancy test you'd done, my first thought was, *This is too soon* and I know I didn't hide that thought very well. At all well. It was clearly written on my face.

'You accused me of not wanting the baby and that wasn't true. I wasn't happy about the timing—' they'd agreed to wait until he'd finished his training, until they had established their careers '—and I was worried about how we'd manage. I was going to be working long hours and studying on top of that. We were away from home, away from

your siblings, away from any of our support
networks. It was going to be tough.

'I knew you were excited and I knew you
wanted me to be excited too and I knew you
were upset with me because it was obvious
that I wasn't. I was scared.'

'Scared?'

He nodded. 'I didn't know how we were
going to manage. I had all sorts of thoughts—
some were premature, I admit. My head went
straight to the nine months ahead. How would
we cope? We had no help. We'd be down an
income. How would I manage to work and
study with a new baby in the house? How
would I support you emotionally and finan-
cially? How would I support a family? I had
no idea how to do it all and that knowledge
terrified me. I knew I would let you down. I
wasn't ready. I wasn't prepared. It was a scenario I wasn't expecting at that point in time
and I accept that I didn't handle it well.'

He'd been convinced that a pregnancy
would derail their plans but Lily had been
adamant that they'd figure it out. He wasn't
so sure. 'I couldn't change my path. I knew
you were going to have to be the one making sacrifices, you would be the one putting
your career on hold.'

'That was a decision I was prepared to make. That I was happy to make,' Lily said.

'I didn't want you to resent me later for continuing with my plans, my career.'

'You would rather I felt like you didn't want our baby?'

'That was never the case. I know things were a little wobbly for a while. You were emotional. I was terrified. But I calmed down, I realised people managed to raise families with a lot less than we had. I realised you were right, we'd figure it out as we went along, and I started to think of all the positives. I loved you—' he still loved her '—and I got excited about the prospect of fatherhood. Of raising a child with you. I went from being scared to being excited. I was still nervous but confident I could do it. That I could support you. That we could raise a child. I thought we got through those first few weeks unscathed. I thought our relationship was back on track. We were building a future.'

What he hadn't realised was that they'd been building a house of cards and when Lily lost the baby their house came crashing down.

'And then we lost the baby. I know you think I didn't grieve but I was trying to stay strong for you. I didn't think it was helpful if we both went to pieces but I can see that by hiding my grief to protect you it appeared that I wasn't grieving at all. I was and I was also dealing with my guilt.'

'Your guilt?'

He nodded. 'You were right, I hadn't been ready for fatherhood initially and that knowledge weighed heavily on my conscience when we lost the baby. I felt we were being punished for my thoughts and I also felt responsible that you'd been put in harm's way. I felt guilty because I let you down. You and our baby. If I hadn't taken the position in London, you wouldn't have been in that situation. If I wasn't working such long hours you wouldn't have been out late at the shops. I felt I should have protected you better. I blamed myself. And whenever I thought you wanted to talk I felt guilty all over again.' And every time Lily looked at him all he could see in her eyes were recriminations.

'I thought you were ignoring our loss,' she said.

'In my mind what happened, happened and there was no way to change that. Talking about it over and over wouldn't change anything.'

'I thought you were ignoring me,' Lily

said. 'I gave up trying to talk to you about it. It was easier to leave.'

'I know I shut you out and I'm sorry. I didn't know how to fix you. I thought you needed to see your sisters. That you needed some sunshine. I thought time would heal your wounds but I always thought you'd come back to me. I assumed we'd be able to put our loss behind us and move on. That we'd get back on track. Our original plan had been to wait until after London before we started a family. I thought we could go back to that plan. I didn't expect not to see you for the next two years. I didn't expect a pandemic to keep us apart. I didn't expect a lot of things. If you could have travelled, would you have come back to me?'

'I don't know. I could have travelled. I wasn't sure if I wanted to. I didn't know if you wanted me back and I wasn't sure if I was ready to see you. You stopped talking to me. You stopped looking at me.'

'All I thought I could see in your eyes was accusations. I didn't want to see my faults, my failings in your eyes.'

'I thought you blamed me,' Lily said.

'Blamed you? No! Getting assaulted wasn't your fault.'

'Not for the assault but for losing the baby.'

'You lost the baby *because* of the assault. Because of the trauma. It wasn't your fault. You shouldn't even have been at the shops.' Otto knew that if he had left the hospital when he was supposed to he would have been the one at the shops, not Lily. He had stayed at work because an interesting case had come in, he'd put his work before his pregnant wife and he still hadn't forgiven himself for that. 'It was my fault, not yours,' he admitted.

CHAPTER SIX

LILY HAD BLAMED him too. Not completely, she knew she couldn't lay all the blame at his feet, but she had certainly laid some of it there.

She'd asked Otto to pick up some tea from the shops on his way home. It was the one thing that helped with her morning sickness, which seemed to strike at any time of the day or night, but Otto had called to say he'd been held up at work so Lily had gone out instead. The shop was two blocks away and despite the cold she'd decided it wasn't worth getting in a taxi, so she'd been walking alone along the dark and icy street when a young man had run past and grabbed at her bag. Lily had held on to it, refusing to let go. Instinct, she'd said later. Stubbornness. She hadn't wanted to let the boy get the better of her. She hadn't thought about the baby. She'd only thought about her bag.

And that knowledge was something she had to live with now.

The thief had pulled hard on her bag but Lily hadn't given in. Not until he'd punched her in the stomach. She'd thought about the baby then as she was doubled over in pain. She'd loosened her grip on her bag and, as the thief yanked it out of her hands, she'd stumbled and slipped on the icy footpath, falling heavily and hitting her head.

Even thinking about it now was still overwhelming. She recalled the shock of the punch, the pain in her abdomen and her absolute fear for her unborn child as she lay bloodied and bruised outside the shop.

Witnesses had come to her aid. She'd sat up gingerly, her hands cradling her belly. She remembered feeling relieved as she'd felt the baby moving. She'd sustained a concussion but she hadn't been concerned about a head injury, her only concern had been for her child, but feeling the movement had convinced her that she'd escaped serious injury. Until the bleeding started and her world imploded.

She'd been rushed by ambulance to the hospital, the sirens and flashing lights adding an extra layer of panic to her fear. She'd prayed to the God she didn't believe in as she was taken to hospital but it had made no difference. The doctor diagnosed a placental abruption and there was nothing that could be done to save her baby.

Whether it was the punch to her stomach or the fall she would never know but her baby paid the ultimate price.

Outwardly, apart from a few bruises, nothing looked amiss but internally, both physically and emotionally, Lily was damaged. She'd never imagined she could lose her baby and she needed someone to bear the brunt of her devastation, someone to absorb her guilt, someone to take the blame.

Otto had become her scapegoat. If he hadn't stayed at work, if he'd come home when he was meant to, she wouldn't have gone to the shops. Eventually, when he began to avoid her, when he refused to talk about the baby or about what they were going to do next, her resentment built into anger.

'I needed you to tell me it would be OK. That it wasn't my fault.' He should have blamed her but she wasn't ready to admit that she felt guilty too. She had been happy to let him shoulder that burden.

'I didn't know that was how you were feeling. You never said anything.'

She shouldn't have needed to. But, deep

down, she knew she was also at fault. Even if the thief had to take the lion's share of the blame she knew she and Otto were both partly responsible due to their actions. She should have just let go of the bag. Why hadn't she? If she'd just let it go everything would have been fine.

But she couldn't go back. She couldn't change her actions.

How she wished she could.

'Lily?' Otto reached out and held her hand. 'I'm sorry I let you down. Can you forgive me?'

She realised she'd reached a place of acceptance and forgiveness. She couldn't continue to blame Otto or herself for what had happened. They were not responsible. The person at fault was the man who assaulted her.

'Yes.' She nodded. 'We could repeat our exact same actions from that night a hundred times and the same situation would never arise. I think I've finally accepted that.'

'Do you think we can try again?'

That was a question she still didn't know the answer to. She was worried he still wasn't ready. That they were still on different tracks. 'We can't just pick up where we left off. We can't go back to how we were before I got pregnant. We're not the same people any more.'

'I know that but that doesn't mean we can't find our way back to each other. We're not beyond saving.'

But she was worried that they were.

Unless he changed his stance about having children she couldn't see the point in staying married. She loved him and she worried she'd never find that type of love again but even though her anger had gone there was still a lot of pain. She could forgive him but she was afraid he could break her heart a second time.

Perhaps it was better to call time on their relationship now.

She looked at their hands, at their intertwined fingers, and remembered what they'd shared. Remembered the love they'd had and wondered if he loved her still. What if she never found love again? Did she want to navigate the world alone?

'Lily? Tell me what you're thinking. Talk to me. Tell me how you're feeling,' Otto implored.

She knew it was time for some honesty. The point of counselling had been to open the lines of communication and she knew there was a lot they needed to talk about, but she also knew she didn't have the energy or the fortitude to begin what would be a difficult conversation. It had already been an emotional day and she was feeling fragile. But there was something she could tell him. 'I don't know what the future holds but I don't want to be alone.'

'Tonight or always?'

'Both.' She knew she wouldn't sleep. She would toss and turn, thinking things over, thinking about today, thinking about their baby, thinking about Otto.

'What can I do?' he asked.

'Will you stay with me until I fall asleep?'

He hesitated and she thought he was going to say no. But he nodded, slowly. 'I'll do the dishes while you get ready for bed.'

Lily chose an old T-shirt, one of her own, and climbed into bed a few moments before Otto joined her. 'Will you lie with me?' she asked. She knew she shouldn't make that request but it might be the last time that she would share a bed with him and she knew that letting him go wasn't going to be easy.

He slid under the covers and lay behind her. She closed her eyes and snuggled back against him as his body moulded around hers and his arms wrapped around her.

She could feel him breathing, she could

feel the rise and fall of his chest and the warm puffs of air against her cheek as he exhaled.

'I'm here. I've got you,' he whispered, and she felt him press his lips to the side of her head, just behind her ear.

Her nerve endings flared under the warmth of his lips. It would be so easy to roll over. To press her lips to his, to taste him, to love him, but she resisted the temptation. They weren't on the same page, not yet, and she would only confuse things, for both of them.

She concentrated on the rhythm of his breathing, matching her breaths to his, letting her heart rate slow and her thoughts quieten, until she slept.

For the first time in weeks Lily woke feeling refreshed. Despite her fears that she wouldn't sleep, that she'd toss and turn and relive the events of the day, and of the day two years ago, she'd slept soundly, dreamlessly, and she knew it was because of Otto.

She shouldn't have let him lie with her but she'd needed comforting and it had felt so good. So familiar. He'd been fully clothed, there had been no hint of anything sexual, she'd fallen asleep almost immediately and had only woken once and when she'd found herself still wrapped in his arms she'd gone straight back to sleep. But he wasn't beside her now. At some time in the night he must have left without her hearing him and she missed him already.

She stretched and rolled over and was lying facing the door, contemplating whether she needed to get up, when Otto walked into the room.

'Good morning,' he said as he placed a cup of tea and a plate beside her bed.

Lily breathed in the scent of freshly buttered toast. 'Good morning.' She'd had no idea that he was still in the house but she was incredibly pleased to see him. 'I didn't realise you'd stayed all night.'

'I didn't want to move in case I disturbed you. You seemed to be sleeping soundly and I think you needed it.'

'It was the best I've slept in ages. I slept like a log.'

'I didn't realise logs snored.'

'I didn't!' she protested.

'No, you didn't.' He smiled at her and her heart melted. How she wished the past two years had never happened. How she wished they could go back in time to before it all went wrong. To when they had their life together in front of them. Oblivious to what was to come, they had lived each day in a state of blissful anticipation, full of the naivety and hopefulness of youth. In the certainty that they were leading charmed lives and they had the world at their feet.

Oh, how those dreams had then shattered into a million tiny pieces leaving her alone to try to salvage what remained. Alone to try to pick up the few bits she could and piece them back together into what became a poor imitation of the life she'd dreamed of. She was still trying to piece it together but the pieces continued to slip through her fingers. She couldn't hold on to them all.

What if Otto was the glue she needed to make things work? To fix things. That would be ironic. He always said anything could be fixed. What if he was the missing piece?

He glanced at his watch. 'I need to get to work. Are you going to be OK?'

With a dozen small words he smashed her brittle illusions.

He wasn't the glue.

He had to go to work.

Work still came before her. Nothing had changed but she knew she shouldn't have expected it to. Not now. Otto didn't owe her anything more. She was the one pushing him away. She was the one who had raised the topic of divorce. What did she expect? That he'd drop everything to stay by her side? She knew she was being unreasonable. She didn't even have time to spend with him today, she had prior commitments that she couldn't get out of, didn't want to get out of.

She nodded in response to his question. 'I'll be fine. I'm spending the day with Poppy and Daisy.' It was the eve of Poppy and Ryder's wedding and the sisters had a full schedule. They were picking up Poppy's wedding dress, going out for lunch and then having pedicures. It was more than enough to keep her mind occupied. In the bright morning light with the cloudless blue sky outside her window it was a new day. She'd be OK.

'And tonight?'

'Girls' dinner with Poppy, Lily and Mei and then Poppy is staying here.' She smiled. 'Something about not wanting Ryder to see her until the ceremony tomorrow. Aren't you supposed to be having drinks with the groom and Jet?'

'I'd forgotten about that with everything else that's happened in the past twenty-four hours,' he said. 'So, I'll see you at the wedding, then?'

She nodded.

'Call me if you need me,' he said before he left, easing her hurt feelings a little.

Perhaps work wasn't the only thing that was important but while she appreciated the offer she knew she wouldn't call. She had to put the past to bed. They'd made mistakes, she'd made mistakes, but there was no going back. She'd forgiven him and now she had to move on.

But last night had left her conflicted. She'd missed their intimacy. She'd missed him. But she couldn't let a few hours spent wrapped in his arms influence her decision if nothing was going to change.

Otto's arms were light, they were missing Lily already, but his heart was heavy. Lily had forgiven him but she wasn't prepared to give him a second chance.

Last night might have been the last time he had the chance to hold her. That was why he'd stayed all night. He couldn't bear to let her go.

But it was safe to say things were not going according to his plan. He needed to work out what was going wrong.

He placed a call to Helen, hoping she had a cancellation and would have time to speak to him.

'Hello, Otto, what can I do for you?'

'I need some advice. Counselling isn't working the way I imagined.'

'How is that?'

Helen always answered a question with another question. It was infuriating but he knew why. It was a technique employed to make them work out the answers for themselves. 'I've shared my letter with Lily but she seems reluctant to tell me how she feels.' He heard the irony in his statement. Having difficulty talking about feelings wasn't something only Lily struggled with. He found it difficult too. Growing up with brothers and then going to a boys' boarding school didn't exactly help to develop the skills needed to share his innermost thoughts. 'I don't know if she is going to let me back into her life. I'm not sure that she's going to change her mind about the divorce. How do I fix this?'

'You might not be able to.'

'I have to. It's what I do.'

'Why is that, do you think?' Helen asked.

'Are you going to make this about me?'

'It's about both of you but, yes, currently it's about what you can do. It's about what you can control.'

'I have to get her to change her mind. I have to find a solution.'

'She might not change her mind. That was something we discussed at your first session. I think when you talk about fixing things you need to think about what you can control. You can't control Lily. You can't control her thoughts or her actions. All you can do is manage your own expectations about how you want your relationship to go.'

'I can't lose her.'

'How do you think Lily got to this point?'

'She feels I let her down.' She'd made that much clear.

'How?'

'I wasn't there when she needed me.'

'It's not Lily's mind you have to change. You can't control that. You can't change the way she feels. She's entitled to her feelings, even if they differ from yours. You have to accept that and work out what you can do. What you can control is what you do going forwards. You need to show Lily that you have her back. She wants a partner. Someone who is there always. Not just through the good times. Yes, she likes your spontaneity and humour. She sees it as a good foil for her more serious personality but she needs to know that you'll be there for her in the tough times. Can you do that?'

Otto nodded. Helen's words resonated

with him and he recognised the truth in them. He knew Lily felt that her parents had let her down. He knew she felt the weight of responsibility of raising her siblings and that she'd looked to him as someone who would share the burden of responsibility, not add to it. He was supposed to take care of her.

He would do better. If Lily would give him a chance.

'Are you ready?' Lily asked Poppy, as the wedding car pulled up on Queen Elizabeth Drive in front of the Bondi Pavilion, opposite the circular Bondi lifeguard tower.

'Definitely.' Poppy smiled. 'I've been waiting a whole lifetime for this moment.'

'You look beautiful,' Daisy signed as the driver opened the door for Poppy and all four siblings climbed out of the car.

Poppy's dress was a simple design, a fitted bodice with narrow straps, that plunged to her waist at the back. The skirt was full from the waist and fell to her ankles, but the simple style was elevated by the fabric, which was adorned with thousands of tiny sequins, which would shimmer and shine in the lights at the evening reception. She carried a bouquet of white poppies interspersed with tiny daisies and lily of the valley in a nod to her sisters. Lily and Daisy were wearing pale blue linen dresses, also sleeveless, which finished mid-calf. All three of them had bare feet in preparation for the beachfront wedding ceremony.

It was just after seven on a mild, late summer evening. The lifeguards had pulled down the shutters on the tower, closing it up for the night. They'd roped off an area in front of the building and had chairs positioned on the beach forming a sandy aisle down the centre of the rows. The wedding guests were mingling but took their seats when they spotted Poppy, leaving Ryder standing at the water's edge waiting for his bride.

Jet, dressed in linen trousers and a pale blue linen shirt to match his sisters' dresses, kissed Poppy's cheek and offered her his arm before they made their way down the steps beside the tower.

Ryder wore a white linen shirt, sleeves rolled up to his elbows, pale linen trousers with the cuffs turned up and bare feet. He was grinning broadly as he watched Poppy walk down the sand towards him.

Lily looked around at the assembled guests as the celebrant welcomed everyone. The guests, a mixture of paramedics, lifeguards, a few of Ryder's new work colleagues and some of Daisy and Lily's hospital colleagues who had befriended Poppy, made a large gathering. Considering neither Poppy nor Ryder had lived in Bondi for long they had made a lot of friends. Mei, Ajay and Otto stood on the left of the aisle with An Na and Niki. They were Poppy's family until she was united with Ryder's, enlarging her family further.

The three dark-haired in-laws were such a striking contrast to the blonde Carlson tribe and the idea of opposites attracting seemed so obviously at play that it made Lily smile. Her gaze landed on Otto, standing so straight, tall, dark and handsome, and her thoughts skipped back to their wedding day, when Otto had been waiting for her at the front of the church his family had attended since before he was born. Otto was watching her and her heart missed a beat when he smiled at her, bringing her back to the present and the recent memory of being wrapped in his arms as she'd fallen asleep. She dropped her gaze as she felt the blush stealing across her cheeks. She was reluctant to let Otto see where her thoughts had gone. She didn't know what to make of her feelings and until she did she didn't want him to attach any significant meaning to last night.

She let her gaze continue to roam over the party. Ryder's parents and younger sister stood with him. His parents were divorced but seemed to have been able to put aside their differences for Ryder's sake. His mother's new partner was among the guests but Lily was yet to meet him. Mei's parents had also been invited but Pete and Goldie Carlson were not on the list. Lily wondered now if Poppy had made the right call by not inviting their parents. Increasingly of late she had been feeling that time was running out. But that was her sentiment, not Poppy's, and she knew it was, at least partly, related to her biological clock.

Lily returned her attention to the ceremony. Poppy and Ryder's vows were heartfelt and sincere and both of them included plenty of references to the family and friends who had gathered to witness the occasion. It was a celebration of Poppy and Ryder's love and the celebrant was well aware of the importance of the guests in the couple's life together.

'Poppy and Ryder are making a commitment to each other here today but all of you are part of that commitment too,' she said. 'By accepting an invitation to their wedding you are making a commitment to support them in their life together. You are promising to be present in their lives, not just for the good times, the weddings, the parties, the celebrations, but for the hard parts too. There is no doubt they will experience difficult times, hopefully these are few and far between, but when they do, your role as friends and family is to support them. Today, you become part of their team as they go forwards into their life together.'

Lily knew how important family was and her thoughts returned to her own. Was their family too badly fractured to be put back together? Their family dynamics had always been unusual—was she wishing for something that was impossible? Even if the siblings' relationship with their parents was repaired, could it ever be the one she imagined? She doubted it.

It wasn't something that had bothered her before. She'd never had a close bond with her parents and her siblings had been enough for her. She knew they would support her as the celebrant was asking them to support Poppy and Ryder but once they had their own families was it realistic to think they could remain as close? Would their partners become their priority? Or the families they would be making together?

That was what she'd hoped to build with Otto. A family of her own. She couldn't expect her siblings to prioritise her over their own families and her parents weren't part of her life. Her family was fractured and she had kept her friends at arm's length since her return from London. Some had been Otto's friends first and she didn't want to see them or answer their questions—she left Otto to deal with that. A lot of her friends were having babies and she found that painful. She didn't want to talk about babies, her marriage or her failure as a mother. But if her siblings had less time to spend with her, where would that leave her? Who would she have for support?

She used to think she had Otto. She knew it was her fault that she didn't have that any more. She knew she'd pushed him away. And then run.

The ceremony was wrapping up and Lily took Poppy's bouquet as the bride and groom exchanged rings.

Poppy was radiant. Lily hadn't ever seen her this happy and she felt a twinge of regret mixed with sadness. She wished her relationship with Otto hadn't gone pear-shaped but she didn't want to be sad, not today. She took a deep breath and reset her attitude as Ryder and Poppy shared their first kiss as husband and wife. She would let Poppy and Ryder's happiness restore her spirits.

The wedding reception was in full swing. The party had all the right ingredients—a gorgeous venue, generous hosts, delicious food, music and guests who were ready to celebrate. Ajay and Daisy had offered to host and Ajay's house was a perfect location. It sat at the opposite end of Bondi from Lily's house, perched on the northern end with an amazing view down the coast. The twinkling lights of Bondi sparkled on the right, the sea was a vast expanse of midnight blue on the left and the curve of the sand in between glowed white in the moonlight. It was magical.

Mei's parents and Ajay's housekeeper-cum-nanny, Mrs Singh, had organised the catering and professional wait staff were kept busy offering platters of food to the guests and topping up glasses. There was nothing for Lily to do except enjoy herself but despite her resolution it wasn't as easy as she would like.

Otto was mingling in the crowd, happily chatting to friends, acquaintances and strangers. It was something he was adept at.

He had always been far more extroverted than Lily. She was happy looking for reasons not to talk to other people, preferring to keep her cards close to her chest, but tonight, Otto's extroverted personality left her feeling ignored. She sighed. What did she expect?

She was acutely aware of where he was at all times and he was currently talking to Poppy's paramedic friends. She watched him, envious of his confidence, and she watched the women he was talking to, aware of the attention Otto was receiving from the female guests. Was she really ready to give him up? The conundrum of her head versus her heart rose again and she turned away, still not a hundred per cent certain she was making the right decision.

The DJ had set up on the deck that looked along the beach towards the centre of Bondi. Ajay had strung festoon lights above the deck and as the dance music started up, guests began to move outside.

Niki, Ajay's two-year-old son, had fallen asleep on a couch near the kitchen and Lily used him as an excuse to escape for a few moments, to give herself some breathing space. She picked him up and carried him to his room. He was sleeping soundly and didn't wake as she got him ready for bed.

She tucked him under his covers and sat with him for a while, thinking about Otto, thinking about their past, thinking about the daughter she and Otto had lost. She would have been about the same age as Niki, just a few months younger. They could have grown up together.

She watched Niki sleep. Watched his chest rise and fall, watched his eyelashes flutter against his cheek, as she pictured her own daughter. Niki was dark, like his father. In Lily's mind her own daughter was always fair-haired, like all the Carlsons, with Otto's dark eyes.

She breathed in and closed her eyes as pain pierced her chest. The heartache was just as acute, just as raw, as it was every time she let the memories surface.

'Lily?'

She opened her eyes, quickly wiping away a tear, when she heard her name.

Otto was standing in the doorway, his lean frame silhouetted by the light from the passage. 'What are you doing sitting in the dark?' he asked her. 'You're missing the party.'

'I just needed a minute,' she said as she got up and joined him in the passage, pulling Niki's door behind her but not shutting it completely.

'Are you OK?' Otto was looking at her closely and she hoped she'd removed all traces of tears from her face.

She nodded. 'Yes. Just reliving the past.' She knew from his expression that he thought she was mad to be looking backwards, so she clarified her answer. 'I was wondering if I should have done things differently.'

'Things like?'

'Whether we should have invited my parents to our wedding.'

'Why on earth are you thinking about that?'

How did she explain? 'I was thinking about what the celebrant said about family. I've seen Mei's parents' relationship with An Na and Niki with Mrs Singh and also Ajay's parents when they visited from Fiji. I never knew my grandparents and seeing my niece and nephew with theirs was the first time I'd really seen what a normal, healthy intergenerational family relationship can look like. When I have children of my own one day I want them to know their grandparents, which made me wonder if my relationship with my parents is irreparable.'

'Of course, it's not,' Otto replied. 'Everything is fixable.'

But she knew that wasn't true. 'I don't know. Family can be complicated. My family is definitely complicated.'

'You won't know until you try,' he said. 'But, for now, come and dance with me. Tomorrow is another day.'

'You're not going to offer me a solution?' she asked, amazed he wasn't trying to fix things immediately.

'I thought you didn't want me to do that any more.'

'Maybe…but I can see on your face that you want to say something.'

Otto grinned and her heart skipped. He really was devilishly handsome when he smiled. 'I was just thinking that if I wasn't already married I'd marry you tomorrow and invite your parents to the wedding. I would insist and you would thank me later.'

'You'd marry me tomorrow?'

'And the next day and the next,' he said as he held out his hand, 'but, right now, we are celebrating with Poppy and Ryder. Come and enjoy the moment. Don't hide away giving the impression that you're miserable. Smile and dance,' he gently reprimanded.

He was right. She had vowed to enjoy herself. To be supportive of her sister and her new husband. She shouldn't be sitting alone in the dark.

'Tomorrow you can go back to wanting to divorce me,' he said with a wink as he took her hand in his.

She let him have her hand, let his fingers close around hers as he led her out onto the deck, let him take her in his arms as the DJ played a slower song. It seemed like all the guests were dancing and the crowded space meant he had to hold her close. She wasn't complaining. When she was in his arms divorce was the last thing she was thinking about.

'I shouldn't have said I *wanted* to divorce you,' she replied. 'I really meant I *needed* to.'

'You're talking in past tense,' Otto said. 'Are you changing your mind?'

Lily didn't know what she was doing. She couldn't think straight. But one thing hadn't changed. 'I feel as if I'm getting left behind,' she said. 'As if I might miss my chance to have children if I wait any longer. I want a family. That's what this is about.' She was envious of her siblings, all happily coupled together and embarking on the rest of their lives while she was in a holding pattern.

She sighed. She had a lot of regrets and

she was worried that letting Otto go might be another one to add to her list but she couldn't see any other way to get what she wanted. She'd missed being with Otto but she would acclimatise.

'For the moment, I am still your family,' he said. His hand was warm on her skin and his voice was a whisper in her ear, sending a tingle along the length of her spine. 'I've missed this.'

She hadn't been honest with him for a long time. Maybe it was time that changed. 'I have too,' she replied.

'Don't let me go,' he said as he pressed his lips to her temple.

Lily's knees went weak and she clung to him for support. 'I won't,' she whispered. 'Not yet.'

He was her husband, her family, but she knew she wouldn't feel her family was complete until she was a mother. But she wanted a night off from thinking about that, from letting herself be consumed by those dreams. She wanted to remember what it was like to be held by her husband. She wanted to spend one more night in Otto's arms. She wanted to share her bed with him, she wanted to feel loved just once more before she said goodbye. But maybe dancing together was as close as she was going to get.

She closed her eyes and concentrated on how it felt, in case it was the last time. She committed every sensation to memory. The warmth of his hand, the touch of his fingers, his familiar scent of cedar and spice, the feel of his shirt against her cheek, the softness of his breath against her forehead and the beat of his heart under her ear.

As Otto held her in his arms and guided her around the dance floor Lily felt the pain of the past two years start to ease. With each beat of the music her spirit lifted as she lost herself in the sensation of being with Otto. Her body felt alive, her heart was light and for a few hours she let herself dream of a future with Otto. A bright, shiny, happy future where they had resolved all their differences.

They stayed on the dance floor until the final song of the evening, until the time came to farewell Poppy and Ryder. The guests crowded around the bride and groom to say goodnight but Lily and Otto found themselves in a corner of the deck, out of the spotlight and out of sight.

'Do you want to say goodbye?' Otto asked.

He still had her hand in his. Lily didn't want to let go, she wasn't ready to break the spell. She didn't want the night to end. She didn't want her dream to give way to reality.

She lifted her head and looked him in the eye as she shook her head. 'In a minute.'

He smiled and held her gaze, his brown eyes dark and intense in the dim light. She was standing still, transfixed. He let go of her hand and she wanted to reach for it, to hold onto it, to hold on to him, but before she could move she felt his arms go around her waist as he pulled her closer to him. One hand was on the bare skin of her back, the heat of his fingers intense against her spine.

His other hand was under her chin. He pressed lightly under her jaw and she tilted her head as her body melted against him.

Otto bent his head and Lily closed her eyes in anticipation of the kiss she was certain was imminent. His lips brushed over hers, the gentlest of touches, so soft she wondered if it was nothing more than her imagination. Was he not sure of the reception he would get?

His mouth met hers again and she welcomed his kiss. His touch was firmer this time, more definite. Her lips parted voluntarily and she heard herself moan as his tongue explored her mouth. The outside world receded; it was condensed into this one spot, this one man.

She was aware of nothing else except the sensation of being fully alive. She wanted for nothing except him.

She felt her nipples harden as all her senses came to life and a line of fire spread from her stomach to her groin. Her heart was racing in her chest as she deepened the kiss. She was dizzy, light-headed, her breaths not deep enough to get oxygen to her brain. She needed to breathe.

Otto's fingers trailed down the side of her cheek sending a shiver of desire through her as they broke apart. He studied her face as if committing each of her features to memory. He didn't need to worry, she thought, she wasn't done with the night yet.

'Why don't you say goodbye to Poppy and I'll give you a lift home?' he asked.

She nodded. She'd let him take her home and she'd invite him in. What happened after that was up to Otto but if he accepted her invitation she knew it would lead to sex. At least she hoped so. She knew she was flirting with danger but it had been so long since she'd had sex and sex with Otto was always good.

The opportunity was hard to resist.

Impossible.

If it happened, she would add it to the memories she was making tonight. It might turn out to be another regret but she wasn't going to think about that now. She'd worry about that tomorrow. What had Otto said? 'Tomorrow is another day.'

He sat in the back of the taxi with her, his arm around her shoulder, holding her close as if he was afraid she would disappear if he let her go. He didn't know she had no intention of going anywhere, not tonight, not without him.

'Would you like to come in?' she asked as the taxi pulled up in front of her house. Their house.

He looked at her, a question in his dark eyes.

She didn't speak, she just nodded.

He paid the fare as she hopped out onto the footpath. The pavement was still warm from the heat of the day under her bare feet and despite the dancing she could feel grains of sand clinging to her calves as she climbed the steps to the front door.

She suspected there was sand sticking to other parts of her body as well.

Otto joined her as she turned the key. She let them into the house and handed him the keys. 'I need a shower, I'm covered in sand,' she said as she headed for the stairs. She climbed two steps before stopping and turning back to him. 'You're welcome to join me.'

CHAPTER SEVEN

SHE WASN'T GOING to play games. She wanted Otto to know where she was at but she'd barely finished the sentence before he was behind her.

She walked up the stairs and, knowing his eyes would be on her hips, she made sure to sway them just a little more.

She walked into her en suite bathroom and stretched her arm out, turning on the taps. While she waited for the water to warm up she undid her bra strap through the thin fabric of her dress and slid her arms out before pulling the bra from inside her dress. She remembered how Otto had always been astonished by her ability to remove her underwear without removing her clothes and she took pleasure in teasing him with that memory now.

She wasn't disappointed with his reaction. He stood, watching her undress, silent but not immobile. She dropped her gaze to his groin. She could see the effect she was having on him and it emboldened her.

'Are you sure about this?' he asked. His voice was husky and deep, laced with desire.

She nodded and he took a step towards her but she held up her hand, making him wait.

She reached back and checked the water temperature before sliding the straps of her dress from her shoulders and letting it drop to the floor. She stepped out of her underwear and stood naked before him. She watched as his eyes darkened as he took in her naked form. His lips parted as he breathed deeply.

Lily smiled and lifted her hands to her hair. She pulled out the pins that had been holding it up, letting it fall around her shoulders before stepping into the shower. She turned her back to him and lifted her face to the spray, letting the warm water run between her breasts, waiting for Otto to join her.

Otto had watched, mesmerised, as Lily's dress slid to the floor. Automatically his eyes had followed the movement as gravity took hold and his gaze was now focused on the dress where it lay in a pool of blue around Lily's ankles. His eyes travelled upwards, up the length of her bare legs, long and tanned, to her slim hips, to the small triangle of blonde hair at the junction of her thighs.

He couldn't speak. A severe lack of blood to his brain had robbed him of the power of speech. But he could admire. So he did. Lily was naked and she was gorgeous.

His gaze travelled higher, over her flat stomach and her round belly button to her full breasts and erect nipples.

She was perfect.

He could see her pulse beating at the base of her throat, her lips were parted, her mouth pink and soft, her eyes gleaming.

She was glorious.

She lifted her hands to her hair and pulled out the pins, dropping them on the vanity as her hair tumbled around her shoulders.

She turned her back and stepped into the shower.

Otto watched her profile as she stood under the spray and lifted her face to the water. His eyes followed the path of the water as it flowed over her breasts and down the length of her thighs. Her skin was tanned and golden with the exception of her bottom, which was pale and smooth and round.

She turned her head, looking over her

shoulder at him, her blue eyes large and wide, watching him as he watched her. She said nothing but when she smiled he couldn't resist any longer. There was only so much temptation he could stand.

He only had one thought. *Do not let her go again.*

He stripped off his clothes as quickly as he could and joined her in the shower.

He hadn't wanted to let her go on the dance floor and he wasn't going to let her go now.

He stepped in behind her and ran his hand over her rounded bottom. Her skin was warm, slick with moisture. She tilted her head to the side and he pressed his lips to the curve of her neck. He moved his hands to her narrow waist, sliding them across her belly and up to her breasts. He ran his thumbs across her nipples, feeling them peak under his touch. His erection hardened further, pressing against her back. He slid one hand down her body, his fingers sliding between her thighs, parting the soft folds of skin between her legs, seeking her centre.

She moaned and leaned back against him, letting him take her weight as her legs could no longer support all of her. He continued to massage her nipple with his left hand as the fingers of his right hand circled the hard little nub of her sex.

She was panting now as she thrust her hips towards him.

'Tell me what you want, Lily.'

He had a good idea of where this was heading but he had to hear her say the words. He had to know she wanted it as much as he did. He didn't want to take advantage of her but he did want to take her. To claim her. To have her. Right here, right now.

Lily's voice was husky and breathless as she replied. 'I want you to make love to me.'

He didn't need to be asked twice.

He spun her around to face him and pulled her close.

It was only a matter of inches before he could bend his head and claim her mouth with his.

Her lips were soft and forgiving under his. He teased them apart with his tongue and she opened her mouth willingly. Her mouth was warm and moist and he felt her arms wind around his neck.

His hands moved lower, cupping her buttocks. She moaned and thrust her hips towards him and he could feel her groin press against his erection. He held her to him, pinning them together.

He nudged his knee between her legs and she spread them apart, willingly, granting him access. His fingers found the centre of her being, as if they had a memory of their own, and he massaged and teased her. She arched her back and he felt her tremble.

'Oh, God, Otto, do it now,' she pleaded.

He scooped her up, lifting her effortlessly. She parted her thighs further and wrapped her legs around his waist as she clung to his shoulders. He thrust into her, deep and smooth, his hands on her hips as he lifted her up and down, sliding her along his shaft.

She tipped her head back, exposing her throat to him, long and slender. But he didn't want to see her throat. 'Look at me,' he commanded.

Their eyes met, unblinking. Her lips were parted.

She bit her bottom lip and closed her eyes.

Her lip came free and she was breathing fast.

She opened her eyes and fixed him with her blue gaze. 'Do it now. Please, Otto.'

She held her breath, only releasing it as she climaxed. He felt her shudder as her hold on him tightened and finally Otto let go as well. He exploded into her soft centre, satisfied and spent for the moment.

He had fought hard to hold on, there had been no slow build up, he'd waited for this moment for two years and it had been hard and fast. He'd take it slow next time, he vowed.

He'd make sure there was a next time.

She clung to him as he turned off the shower. He never wanted to let her go.

He reached out and grabbed a huge, fluffy towel and wrapped it around them both.

He carried her to her bed, refusing to put her down despite her protests. She was long and lean and sexy as hell and he was going to make love to her again. If she'd let him.

The towel fell away as he laid her on the bed. Her skin was shiny, warm and slick. He could feel his desire stirring again and knew he wasn't finished.

He rested his hand on her stomach and his fingers spanned her waist as he bent his head and took her breast in his mouth. Lily breathed in sharply, a little gasp of air, and arched her back, lifting herself closer to him.

He flicked his tongue over her taut nipple before he lifted his head and said, 'I don't think we're done yet.'

Lily wrapped her hand around his erection in silent reply as she opened her legs and guided him inside her. Otto closed his eyes and lost himself in the heady sensation of being with Lily.

They made love slowly this time, savouring each moment. Sex between them had always been amazing, something that two years apart hadn't changed. If anything, it made it sweeter.

They climaxed together for the second time. Spent. Satisfied. Exhausted.

Otto fell asleep pressed against Lily's back with one hand cupping her breast and her head resting against his shoulder. He held her close, never wanting to let her go.

Now he was home.

Lily woke to the sensation of Otto's lips on her cheek. She smiled as she opened her eyes, anticipating a satisfying start to the day. 'Good morning.'

'Good morning, sorry to wake you,' Otto apologised as Lily felt her expectations being dashed. 'I need to go and work on my presentation for the conference.'

'Now?' she asked. The conference was scheduled to start tomorrow afternoon. She would have thought he would have sorted out his talk already.

He nodded and kissed her again, on the lips this time, which sort of made up for the fact that he was heading out of the door. 'I'd love to stay,' he said, bolstering her spirits, 'but I have to get this done. Although I have a suggestion. I thought we could head up to the Hunter Valley later today, take the wine train. Have a night in the resort before the conference starts.'

'Together?'

'Yes, together.'

Lily wondered what door she'd opened by sleeping with him. Was it closure she was after or a second chance? If it was closure she was after then going away with him was probably not the best idea. She wasn't sure what she wanted any more but she had a ready-made excuse, which might buy her some time to figure things out. 'I've got lunch with my siblings today.' Poppy and Ryder had checked into a hotel for their wedding night before they left on their honeymoon and the Carlson siblings were catching up for lunch first.

'The train doesn't leave until four,' Otto said, refusing to be dissuaded. 'You have lunch with your siblings. I'll book two train tickets and pick you up on the way to the station.'

'Do you really think that's a good idea?'

'No. I think it's a great idea,' he said as

he sat on the side of her bed. 'We can spend some time together without interruption. You promised to give me three months, we've got another two. Think of all the fun we can have.' He placed his hand on her knee and his thumb rested on the soft skin on the inside of her thigh. He dragged his thumb slowly towards his fingers and Lily's nerve endings trembled under his touch as her eyelids fluttered. 'I can spend the next two months convincing you not to divorce me and you can spend the time seeing if you can resist me. You know we're good together.'

'It's not that simple,' she said as she resisted the urge to grab him and pull him into bed with her. Resisted the urge to let her actions make a mockery of her words.

'It is that simple,' he replied as his hand slid further up her leg. 'You'll see.' Lily's breathing was slow and deep and she fought hard to keep her eyes open. Fought hard to stop herself from begging him to come back to bed. He was grinning, obviously totally aware of the effect he was having on her. 'I'll pick you up at three.'

Lily loved a plan but Otto had always been able to get her to go with the flow. He was the only one who had ever been able to convince her to wing it and she loved his spontaneity. It was such a good foil for her seriousness. She trusted him to bring the fun and he was right, it was only a couple of days in the Hunter Valley that he was asking for and she had promised to give him a couple more months.

She smiled slowly, deciding to let him convince her, hoping she wasn't making a mistake. 'OK, I'll see you at three.'

Otto congratulated himself on getting Lily to agree to come away with him. He was hoping to remind her of the good times they'd shared. To remind her of all the reasons why she shouldn't divorce him and, after last night, he was convinced that if she gave him enough time he'd be able to win her back. He needed to get her away from other distractions—work especially. He was doing his best to follow Helen's advice. To give Lily what she needed.

He was convinced that what she needed was him and he just needed time to show her that.

They were on board the wine train. Lily was flicking through a magazine reading while Otto worked on his presentation. He was having a final check and was about to suggest they go to the dining car for a glass of wine when a man burst through the connecting doorway into their railcar.

'Is there a doctor? We need a doctor. Is anyone a doctor?' The man ran through the carriage, looking left and right as he shouted, but he didn't stop.

Otto stood up and put his hand out, waylaying the man. 'I'm a doctor. What is it? What's happened?'

'There's a lady in the next car. I think she's having a heart attack.'

Otto closed his laptop and picked it up as Lily stood. 'We'll come with you,' he told the man.

They followed him out of their carriage and as the door into the adjacent carriage slid open Otto could hear the sound of a person in distress. They passed rows of passengers who looked to either be trying to pretend nothing untoward was happening or craning their heads, not bothering to hide their curiosity, as they tried to see the cause of the disturbance.

The woman's cries got considerably louder and as Otto got closer he saw she was clutching her chest as she sat doubled over in pain. She was in an aisle seat, effectively trapping the other passenger against the window. The passenger beside her looked as though he'd rather be anywhere else.

'Are you travelling together?' Otto asked the man beside the woman.

The passenger shook his head, eyes wide. Otto could have guessed by his terrified expression that the woman was a stranger to him and he had no idea what was going on. He wasn't going to be able to give Otto any details.

The woman looked to be in her mid-fifties, moderately overweight and her skin had an unhealthy pallor. Otto's immediate thought was that she was having a heart attack even though it could be any number of things.

Otto looked for the emergency stop button before wondering about the wisdom of pulling that when he had no idea where they were. The view out of the window was of countryside, barely a house or a shed could be seen. He turned to the young man who had alerted him to the patient. 'I need you to go and find a staff member. I need a first-aid kit, whatever they've got, and I need to know how far we are from a hospital.' The young man didn't move. 'Go that way.' Otto pointed in the direction opposite the one they had come from. 'There'll be someone in the dining car.' The man nodded and took off and Otto turned back to the patient.

He introduced himself and Lily, explaining they were both doctors before asking, 'Can I examine you?'

She nodded, unable to speak. Despite the noise she was making it was obvious she was struggling to breathe. Otto needed to calm her down. If her airways were compromised she needed to conserve her energy. Crying was using precious energy that could be better spent trying to force air into her lungs.

'Do you have any history of cardiac problems?' he asked, aiming for questions that only required yes/no answers.

She shook her head but Otto knew that didn't mean he could rule out a heart attack. People didn't necessarily know they were a candidate for a heart attack before they had one.

Lily had her fingers on the woman's wrist, feeling her pulse. 'Rapid but regular,' she told him.

Treating a patient in an emergency outside a hospital environment was not easy, despite what television shows might imply. The risk of dying increased dramatically outside a hospital setting. He wasn't a miracle worker but he'd recently lost a patient and he did not want to be in that position again so soon.

The young man returned with a rail employee. Her name badge read 'Carys' and she was carrying a small black bag that Otto assumed was the first-aid kit, although he'd been hoping for something a little larger.

'How far are we from a hospital?' he asked her as she handed him the bag. They'd been on the train for over an hour, they were well out of Sydney but Otto had no idea of their exact location or what medical care was nearby.

'We're twenty-five minutes from the nearest town with a hospital. We can stop the train but the nearest ambulance will be in that same town.' Which meant there wasn't much point in stopping. The train was travelling at speed. They were better off continuing to move. 'Do you want to stop? Do you know what's wrong?'

No and no were his answers but he didn't want to sound too defeatist. 'Not yet,' he replied, as he unzipped the first-aid kit, wondering how well it would be stocked. Would it have anything useful in it? He couldn't afford *not* to check it out. He had nothing with him.

A list of medications was taped inside—

anti-nausea medication, nitro-glycerine tab-
lets, an EpiPen and a bronchodilator inhaler
were all listed and he committed those items
to memory.

'Can you clear everyone from the car?' he
asked Carys. He didn't need bystanders especially when there was no one who could
give him any helpful information.

He pulled out a stethoscope and a blood
pressure monitor, hoping the battery was
charged. A thermometer lay underneath.

He handed the blood pressure cuff to Lily
and she wrapped it around the patient's upper
arm before inflating it.

'I'm just going to listen to your breathing,'
he told the woman as he slipped the buds of
the stethoscope into his ears and held the
bulb over her shirt. He glanced at the blood
pressure monitor, surprised to find that both
her blood pressure and pulse were within
normal limits for a middle-aged woman. His
gut instinct had been that she was suffering a
heart attack but her heart wasn't going crazy.
That was good news, but her cries of discomfort coupled with the crackling of her shirt
was making it impossible to hear any breath
sounds through the stethoscope.

'I need to slide this under your shirt,' he
explained as he slipped the stethoscope be-

tween her chest wall and her shirt, but the change in position didn't elicit the result he was after. There were still nil airway sounds.

Her skin was turning slightly grey and Otto was concerned.

He assumed there would be a defibrillator on the train but these were only useful in a cardiac arrest, and then only sometimes. A heart attack was a different ball game. The woman was conscious and breathing so a cardiac arrest was unlikely. A heart attack was still his first thought but he knew other conditions could be causing chest pain and shortness of breath. A cold, indigestion, asthma, pneumonia or a virus were all possibilities.

Lily was quietly gathering as much information as she could without a verbal history. She was pointing the thermometer at the patient's forehead—the reading was normal, so Otto crossed pneumonia and a severe virus off the list. By a process of elimination he narrowed the problem down to one of two things: an asthma attack or a heart attack. They weren't similar in presentation but her symptoms weren't really typical for either.

He still wasn't sure that it *wasn't* a heart attack. It was impossible to get any history from her and yes/no questions were only going to get him so far.

'What do you think's going on?' Lily asked.

'It looks like a heart attack and unless I can stabilise her we'll have to call an ambulance and stop the train.'

'What do you need?'

'I'd like an emergency department. I'd like to be able to do an ECG. But I'll have to treat her with what we've got and see what happens.'

He turned to Carys. 'Can you call an ambulance? Find out where they can meet us. We should assume we're going to need them.'

The young girl nodded. 'I'll have to go and find out exactly where we are.'

Otto nodded as Lily asked him, 'That device you were telling me about, the one you're discussing at the conference, that records a heart tracing and sends it to your phone, have you got that in your luggage?'

'Yes.' He'd completely forgotten about the machine. 'You are brilliant.' In this situation having that machine at his disposal was more than he could have wished for.

'Do you want me to get it?'

He'd only ever used it in a training environment but it was the worth a shot. It should give him an idea of what the woman's heart was up to. He nodded. 'It's in my bag on the overhead luggage rack.'

While Lily was gone he took a nitrate tablet from the first-aid kit and slipped it under the patient's tongue, deciding to treat her as a heart attack patient in the interim. If she wasn't having a heart attack the tablet wouldn't do any harm and if her symptoms didn't ease he could administer the bronchodilator inhaler to open up her airways. Again, that wouldn't cause any problems if it wasn't required and he had to do something.

He'd just given his patient two puffs of the inhaler when Lily returned with the portable device. Otto attached the leads, syncing it with his phone, which was in his pocket.

The trace was normal.

It still didn't exclude a heart attack but it did reduce the urgency of treatment and Otto's diagnosis was now leaning towards asthma. As he let out a sigh of relief, his patient started to stabilise. Her breathing slowed, she opened her eyes, unclenched her hands and was able to speak, albeit with difficulty.

She reported a history of severe asthma and the effort of saying a few words brought on further shortness of breath. Otto handed her the inhaler as he listened again to her chest and this time he heard breath sounds.

'Do you have an inhaler?' he asked, thinking it was unusual for an asthmatic patient not to carry one with them.

Maria, she'd said her name was, replied, 'I do but I used it in the taxi on the way to the train station and I think I must have left it on the seat when I paid the fare. I couldn't find it in my bag when I needed it.'

Lily rechecked Maria's blood pressure and pulse and announced they were both closer to normal limits. Otto was confident that Maria's symptoms were asthma related but he insisted on sending her to hospital just to be thorough. He was satisfied with the outcome as he and Lily handed Maria's care to the paramedics. They had worked in unison, their skills complemented each other, and as the ambulance departed Otto's thoughts returned to the previous evening. He and Lily had been in unison then too. He was beginning to feel optimistic about the future. Surely Lily had to agree that their relationship was worth saving? That their marriage was worth fighting for?

'That wasn't quite the start I envisaged for our mini-break,' Otto said as they checked into the hotel.

'I don't imagine it was, but Maria was lucky you were there,' Lily said as the receptionist handed her the room keys. Otto had been given Leo's room but they'd cancelled the booking, agreeing that two rooms were unnecessary. 'We never got that drink on the train,' she said as Otto picked up their bags. 'Shall we have one on the terrace?' Past the reception desk she could see a terrace, which overlooked an ornamental lake and the eighteenth hole of the golf course that was part of the resort where the conference was being held.

'Maybe later,' he replied. 'I've got other things planned for us now. Starting with a massage for you.'

'Really?' she asked. 'Is there a day spa here?'

'I assume so but that's not where you're going. I thought I'd be your masseur.'

He was smiling at her, confident she wouldn't refuse his offer. And he was right. His massages were the best. His surgeon's hands were skilful, supple and strong, able to find all the right spots to achieve the desired outcome. Which Lily knew was sex. His massages always ended in lovemaking. A massage from Otto had always been one of her favourite forms of foreplay.

They found their room and Otto hung the 'do not disturb' sign on the door before closing it. He laid a towel on the bed while Lily lifted her hair and pulled it into a ponytail and then a bun, getting it out of the way. She knew Otto would loosen it again later. He loved to run his fingers through her hair and she had no objection.

She wondered if this was wise. Letting herself knowingly be seduced again. But she wasn't going to put a stop to the interlude. Why deprive herself of pleasure?

She reached for the zip at the side of her dress and undid it slowly. She slipped one strap from her shoulder and then the other and let the dress fall to the floor.

Otto's eyes were dark and intense now. All traces of lightness had vanished as he watched and waited for her.

She reached her hands behind her back and unhooked her bra, sliding it along her arms and dropping it to the floor.

She turned her back and bent forwards, removing her underwear before lying face down on the bed, head turned to one side. Otto draped a towel over her hips and buttocks, covering her legs.

A fan spun lazily overhead and the movement of cool air on her skin brought tiny goosebumps out on her arms. Then Otto's warm hands were on her skin. Running over her shoulders and down her spine. Back up to her shoulders and along her arms. The pressure of his palms and fingers was light to begin with, feather-light. Teasing her and creating goosebumps for a different reason now.

His pressure intensified as he ran his thumbs up alongside her spine. First one side, then the other, finishing at the base of her skull. He massaged the individual muscles around her shoulder blades, then her arms, before returning to her shoulders.

His hands moved out wider, out to the curve of her ribs. His fingers brushed the sides of her breasts and she felt her nipples peak in response. His hands moved lower, to the small of her back, to the little dimples at the top of her pelvis where the bones joined her spine.

He flipped the towel, drawing it off her hips to cover her back, exposing her buttocks and legs. He worked on one buttock, then the other. Kneading in small circles. His hands moved down her legs. First left, then right. He bent her knee and massaged her calf, then foot. Left foot, right foot, back up the right calf. He found tiny knots in her calf and worked them until they were free.

He rested her leg on the bed and moved

her knees apart. His hands were on either side of her left knee now, his fingers splayed on the inside of her thigh. The nerves in her thigh trembled at his touch, igniting a spark of desire that shot deep into her belly. She forced herself to lie still, knowing the anticipation was almost as delightful as the fulfilment that was coming her way.

His thumbs pressed into her hamstring as he ran his hands up the back of her thigh, only stopping at the point where her thigh met her groin. His fingers brushed the gap between her thighs and Lily's stomach twitched in response. She could feel the moisture gathering between her legs. She wanted to push herself against his hand but before she could move his fingers had slipped across her sex and he was now running his hands down her right leg, back to her knee to start all over again on the other side.

She moved her leg slightly wider, giving him more room. She was breathing heavily now and struggling to stay still.

He flipped her over and ran his hand up the inside of her thigh. Lily closed her eyes as her knees dropped apart and Otto slid one finger inside her. She could feel she was wet and warm. Swollen. Ripe.

His thumb found her sex and circled it slowly. Lily arched her hips and pushed herself towards him. But she didn't want to come this way. She wanted him inside her.

She lifted one hand and placed it on his chest. 'Wait,' she said as she sat up. 'I want to do this together.'

She could see he was as eager as she was. His erection strained against his trousers. She reached for him, sliding her hands under his T-shirt. She trailed her fingernails lightly over his skin and heard him moan. She held onto the bottom of his shirt and stood up, pulling his shirt over his head, exposing his flat, toned stomach.

His hands moved to the button on his trousers but Lily was faster. She snapped open the button and slid the zip down. She could feel the hard bulge of his erection pressing into her, straining to get free.

He stepped out of his shoes, not bothering to untie the laces, as she pushed his trousers to the floor. They joined his shoes and shirt in an untidy heap. He was naked except for his boxer shorts. Lily slid them down and Otto stepped out of them. Her eyes travelled over him.

He was glorious.

He grinned at her and winked. He knew

he looked good and he was confident enough to admit it. His confidence was sexy. He was sexy. Lily suspected she would never meet another man who could send her pulse sky-rocketing with just a wink and smile as Otto could. When he was standing before her, gloriously naked and clearly admiring her in the same way, she wondered if getting divorced was the stupidest idea she'd ever had. Was she making a huge mistake? Was Daisy right? Was Otto the only man for her or was it just her hormones making her second-guess herself?

Well, either way, she wasn't backing out of this opportunity, she thought as she took his hand and pulled him onto the bed.

She lifted her hand to pull the elastic from her hair.

'Let me do that.' Otto's voice was husky with desire. Lust coated his words, making them so heavy they barely made it past his lips.

She dropped her hand, leaving her hair restrained. He reached for her hair and pulled the elastic free. He wound his fingers through her hair, loosening the strands as he spread her hair out, letting it fall over her shoulders before burying his face in it.

His fingers rested at the nape of her neck

and his thumb rested on her jaw. It was warm and soft, his pressure gentle. He ran his thumb along the line of her jaw and then his thumb was replaced by his lips. He kissed her neck, her collarbone and the hollow at the base of her throat where her collarbones met.

His fingers blazed a trail across her body that his mouth followed. Down from her throat to her sternum, over her breast to her nipple. His fingers flicked over the nipple, already peaked and hard. His mouth followed, covering it, sucking, licking and tasting.

The fingers of his other hand were stroking the inside of her thigh. She parted her legs and his fingers slid inside her. His thumb rolled over her clitoris, making her gasp. He kissed her breast, sucking at her nipple as his thumb teased her. She arched her back, pushing her hips and breasts towards him, wanting more, letting him take her to a peak of desire.

Still she wanted more. She needed more.

She rolled towards him and pushed him flat onto his back. She sat up and straddled his hips. His erection rose between them, trapped between their groins. He lifted his head, taking her breast into his mouth once more. She closed her eyes as she gave herself up to the sensations shooting through her as his tongue flicked over her nipple. Every part of her responded to his touch. Her body came alive under his fingers and his lips and her skin burned where their bodies met.

She lifted herself clear of him, pulling her breast from his lips. Air flowed over her nipple, the cool temperature contrasting with the heat of his mouth. She put her hands either side of his head and kept her eyes on his face as she lifted herself up and took him inside her. His eyelids closed and she watched him breathe in deeply as her flesh encased him, joining them together.

She filled herself with his length before lifting her weight from him and letting him take control. His thumbs were on the front of her hips, his fingers behind her pelvis as he guided her up and down, matching her rhythm to his thrusts, each movement bringing her closer to climax.

She liked this position. She liked being able to watch him, she liked being able to see him getting closer and closer to release. His eyes were closed but his lips were parted, his breathing was rapid and shallow, his thrusts getting faster.

She spread her knees, letting him in deeper

inside her until she had taken all of him. Her body was flooded with heat. Every nerve ending was crying out for his touch.

'Now, Otto. Now.'

He opened his eyes and his dark gaze locked with hers as he took her to the top of the peak.

Her body started to quiver and she watched him as he too trembled. He closed his eyes, threw his head back and thrust into her, claiming her as they climaxed together.

When they were spent she lay on him, covering his body with hers. Their skin felt warm and flushed from their effort and they were both panting as he wrapped his arms around her back, holding her to him. She could feel his heart beating against her chest. She could feel it as its rhythm slowed, gradually returning to normal.

She tipped her head back and kissed him. 'That was some massage. Thank you.'

'My pleasure. Does this mean you're not going to divorce me?'

'Not today.' She smiled.

CHAPTER EIGHT

OTTO STEPPED OFF the podium at the end of his presentation and made his way to where Lily waited at the back of the room.

'Congratulations, that went well,' Lily said. He was an impressive public speaker. He knew his topic and had the confidence, charm and charisma to hold an audience.

'Thanks, I always prefer to get it out of the way early and then I can enjoy myself,' he said as he walked beside her and out into the foyer. 'Speaking of enjoying ourselves, what are you doing for lunch? Do you want to play hooky with me for the rest of the day?'

'You're not going to stay for any of the afternoon sessions? Some of them sound interesting.'

His expression implied that he had other things on his agenda and his next words confirmed that. 'Some of them do sound interesting but they're all being recorded, which means we can watch them later. There's no roll call, there are no exams,' he said when he could see her wavering. 'No one is going to notice or care if we're here or not. Half the doctors will be playing golf.'

'You want to play golf?' she said. 'That sounds horrendous!' Playing hooky went against the grain for her and if she was going to miss the conference, it needed to be for a better reason than a round of golf. A *much* better reason. Another massage, for instance, could persuade her.

'No,' he laughed. 'I do not want to play golf. I want to take you on a picnic.'

'A picnic?' She'd been hoping for something a little more R-rated. Was it terrible that she was slightly disappointed?

'Do you have a better suggestion?' he asked with a half-smile, making her blush. 'It's a shame to waste such a glorious day by being inside at either the conference or in our room, I'll make it up to you later.'

Lily grinned back at him. 'In that case, then, a picnic sounds like fun.'

Otto called an Uber and had it drop them at a winery that sat at the top of a hill a short distance from the conference resort. He collected a rug and a picnic basket from the cellar at the restaurant and took her across the lawns to a spot out of sight of the winery buildings but with amazing views over the Hunter Valley.

'Did you arrange this in advance?' Lily asked as Otto spread the blanket on the ground.

'I did.'

'Were you that confident I'd say yes?'

'I was pretty confident.' He grinned and took her hands and pulled her down onto the blanket beside him. 'And now,' he said as he opened a bottle of wine and poured two glasses, 'I intend to spend the afternoon reminding you of all the reasons why you don't want to divorce me.'

She never *wanted* to divorce him, she just didn't think she had another option if she wanted a family, but the more time they spent together, the more difficult she found it to imagine her life without him in it. But she was mindful of falling under his spell, of letting herself get swept away by the intimacy and company without thinking about the consequences. Without sorting out their issues.

He had been honest with her, now it was her turn. She needed to clear the air otherwise she knew they wouldn't be able to move forwards.

'There's something I need to tell you,' she said, 'in the interest of full disclosure.'

'Should I be worried?'

'No. It's about the letters Helen asked us to write. I think I need to read you mine.' She'd started writing it as soon as Helen had suggested it. As much as she hadn't been certain it was a good idea, she hadn't considered *not* doing it, but she had found it difficult. She'd stopped and started and hadn't completed it until after Natalie had been admitted to hospital with placental abruption. Until after the night she had spent sleeping in Otto's embrace. Until *after* she'd forgiven both Otto and herself. She'd needed to find forgiveness before she could find closure.

'Putting words on paper made me realise a few things about our relationship. I still think our issues started when I got pregnant but we were both to blame for the failings in our marriage and I needed to accept that some of the fault lay with me. You weren't as excited as I was when I got pregnant, I knew that, and I felt like I was going through the pregnancy on my own. You were busy, focused on your work and study, and we spent very little time together. I knew the timing of the pregnancy wasn't ideal but I felt like you were disengaged and choosing work over me. I knew you were going to be busy while we were in London, that was the whole point of going, but once I got pregnant I expected things to be different and I was upset that they weren't. And then after the assault things got worse. We spent almost no time together and we weren't communicating at all and I realise now there are things I should have told you. Things I should have said. After the assault I was distraught but I was also angry and I took that out on you. For a long time I blamed you. For staying at work instead of coming home. For not comforting me. For not supporting me.'

Otto shook his head. 'You were right to blame me. I did all those things and I've regretted each and every one of them.'

'No, it wasn't fair. We both made mistakes but those mistakes weren't the reason I lost the baby. The man who assaulted me caused that but it was easier to blame you than to accept that I had failed.'

'I don't understand. Why do you think you failed? What mistakes did you make? What did you do?'

'It's what I *didn't* do. I didn't let go of my bag. I should have. I don't know why I didn't. A stupid reflex. Stubbornness. Surprise. Something made me hold on to it but if I'd just let go, he would have left me alone. I wouldn't have been physically assaulted; I wouldn't have fallen. I would have just been a victim of a bag theft instead of a victim of assault. I would have been a woman who lost her bag instead of a mother who lost her baby.' Silent tears rolled down her cheeks and she brushed them away impatiently. She didn't want to look as if she was asking for sympathy. She was admitting her part in the trauma, she was taking responsibility.

'Lily, no.' Otto reached out and wiped the traces of tears from her face and Lily's heart skipped a beat. 'None of what happened was your fault. You don't know that you wouldn't have fallen. He still could have pushed you, punched you, hurt you.'

'I know that now but at the time I felt like I'd failed as a wife and mother and that was hard to deal with.'

'I had no idea you felt like that. Why didn't you say anything?'

'I was afraid of how I felt. Guilty. Lost. A failure. I was scared that if I didn't keep quiet I'd find myself admitting to those emotions and then you'd blame me. I wanted you to comfort me. To tell me you still loved me.

To tell me the placental abruption wasn't my fault. But I was afraid you wouldn't tell me that and I couldn't stand the thought that you'd agree with me. That you'd think I caused our daughter's death.'

'Lily! I never thought that.'

'I could see it in your eyes. You couldn't even look at me.'

Otto shook his head. 'That was my guilt you could see. I thought it was reflected back at me every time I looked at you and it ate away at me. That's why I avoided coming home. That's why I avoided you. Because I couldn't bear to think I'd let you down. I don't blame you. Believe me, if I could go back and have that day again I would do things differently, we both would, but the blame lies with the man who assaulted you, not with you. If he hadn't snatched your bag, if he hadn't pushed you, it would have just been a night like any other. A night when I got home late and you were annoyed with me but we would have forgotten all about it.'

'I know that now,' she said, knowing he was right. It had taken her a long time but she'd forgiven Otto, she'd forgiven herself. 'But I still owe you an apology. I wasn't being honest about my feelings.'

'It doesn't matter...' he began to say before Lily joined in. 'What's done is done,' they said in unison.

Otto smiled and took her hand. 'What does matter is that I love you. I always have and I always will. What does matter is I don't want a divorce. I should have supported you then and I promise to support you now. Will you give me a chance to make it up to you?'

'What are you suggesting?'

'That we give our marriage another shot. Properly. I move back in and we start again. What do you think?'

Was this the moment she'd been waiting for? The moment when forgiveness of their past mistakes, the mistakes that had torn them apart, would turn into a second chance? A chance of a future together?

There was no way of knowing unless she was prepared to take that chance. Unless she was prepared to trust Otto.

She took a deep breath and nodded. 'I think that sounds perfect.'

Otto pulled her to him and kissed her. His kiss tasted of dreams and promises and Lily prayed that this time they would be fulfilled.

He topped up their glasses and proposed a toast. 'Here's to us and our happiness together. We have another life in front of us, we can learn from our past but not let it define our future.'

Lily touched her glass against Otto's and smiled as she pictured that future and the children she was sure were going to be a part of it. 'To our future.'

Lily and Otto walked into Helen's office and for the first time Lily knew she was smiling as they entered. Unlike the previous sessions, today's appointment wasn't filling her with dread. For the first time in months, she was completely happy and she was looking forward to advising Helen that this would be their final session. Otto had moved out of the hotel and back into the house. Their house. And she was enjoying the rebuilding phase of their relationship. She was enjoying having someone to have dinner with, someone to exercise with and someone to share her bed with.

She and Otto were back on track, she thought as she sat on the small sofa beside her husband.

'Is my job done?' Helen asked as they sat. 'You're giving your marriage another chance?'

'Why do you say that?'

'Your body language has changed. You

look more relaxed, Lily, less wary. You're sitting much closer to Otto and you haven't picked up a pillow to put on your lap,' Helen said with a smile.

She was right. In all the previous sessions Lily had felt the need to use a pillow as a barrier, some protection against the attraction she still felt for Otto. But she didn't need that protection any more. She was embracing that attraction. She was embracing their relationship.

'We've made some progress.' Otto smiled.

'You're having sex?'

Lily looked sideways at Otto and smiled as Otto answered for them both. 'Yes.'

'You've resolved all your differences?' Helen asked. 'You've had an open and honest discussion about what went wrong?'

They both nodded.

'That's good. Have you talked about what happens next for you both?' Helen continued. 'What you want your future to look like?'

Lily shook her head. They'd talked about the past and the present but expected the future to take care of itself.

'I assume everything will go back to the way it was,' Otto replied.

'Which was?' Helen asked.

'We spend some time together, just the

two of us, making up for the past two years, getting our relationship back on track. Once we're back on track and our careers are established, then we start trying for a baby.'

Once again, they were at cross purposes and Lily could see her plans crashing down around her. She'd assumed they'd be starting a family now. She'd made assumptions. Perhaps that was a mistake. She turned to Otto. 'You know I want children now. Isn't that what our renewed relationship is all about?'

'You haven't discussed this?' Helen sounded dumbfounded.

'I assumed we were on the same page,' Lily said. She turned to Helen. 'How do we resolve this?' she asked.

'It sounds like you still need to work on open channels of communication,' Helen told them. 'It's a positive that you are still physically attracted to each other and while that's great, sex is an important part of an intimate, monogamous relationship, sex without emotional connection is just sex,' she said. 'Sexual chemistry is important but it isn't enough if you don't share the same goals and similar values. You need to acknowledge that your feelings can, and will, differ from each other and you need to acknowledge that is OK. It's impossible for two people to think and feel exactly the same way about things. You need to respect those differences.

'If a relationship is going to work you should expect to share similar views and goals, but to expect someone else to always share your views on everything is unrealistic. If a relationship is going to work you should be able to deal with challenges together. You don't have to agree on everything but at the end of the day your fundamental beliefs have to align. It's up to both of you to work out what the fundamentals are. You have to decide which differences you are prepared to accept if a relationship is going to last and which differences are non-negotiable. You can walk away without having those conversations but if you want to give your relationship a chance, even if it's being able to move forwards with a different type of relationship between the two of you, then you need to have conversations around that. What are your non-negotiables?'

'I want children,' Lily said.

'So do I,' Otto replied, 'but not yet.'

'When?'

'I assumed we'd wait until you turned thirty-one before we started trying for a family,' Otto replied. 'Just like we'd planned.'

'That's another year away! You know I want children now. We both know that a previous placental abruption increases the risk of having another. I want to try to fall pregnant before I get much older in case something else goes wrong.'

'Lily, I want to be around when we have children. After being sent to boarding school I promised myself that I wouldn't be an absent father. Right now I'm establishing my career. We agreed to wait until you were thirty-two before we had a family. That means aiming to get pregnant next year. I want to be around to help with our children.'

'I can manage.'

'But I don't want you to manage on your own. I want to be there to form that bond.'

'There will never be the perfect time,' Lily retorted. 'There is always something else you want to do, another box to tick, another challenge to meet. What if you keep putting it off?' She was worried he'd keep delaying. She was worried he'd want to wait for ever.

'Marriage is about compromise,' Helen told them. 'Who is willing to compromise?'

Lily wasn't sure if she was. She knew the compromise would be at the expense of an imminent pregnancy and that might be more than she was prepared to give up.

She reached for her bag and stood up. 'I need some time to think about this,' she said. She needed some fresh air, time to clear her head.

'Lily, wait.' Otto had followed her out of Helen's office and he stuck his arm out as the lift doors were closing. 'I'm not letting you go again,' he said as he followed her into the lift. 'We need to sort this out. You want trust. I want truth. I don't want a divorce. I don't want someone else making a family with you. I love you. I always have.'

The lift doors slid closed and Otto faced her. 'If you don't love me, tell me now. If you want a divorce, tell me now. If you want to give our marriage another chance, tell me now and we'll figure this out. Today. We can't get the last two years back but we can have a future. If you don't want a future with me, tell me now, and I will walk away and you can get on with your life.'

The idea of watching Otto walk away made her feel physically ill.

'I don't want someone else to be the father of my children either. I love you too. I don't want a divorce but I do want a baby. If we stay together I can't understand the point of waiting. And I'm worried that you'll keep delaying starting a family.'

'I think we need some time where it's just the two of us. I don't want the added pressure of you trying to get pregnant while I'm starting this new job,' he said. 'I want the next pregnancy to be different from last time. I want to be there to support you through it. I don't want to be at work all the time. I don't want you to feel like you're doing it on your own. Not the pregnancy part. Or the raising our baby part, but I'm willing to compromise. Instead of waiting until next year, can you give me until the middle of this year and then we'll start trying to get pregnant? That's only a few more months. We could have a baby by the middle of next year and I'd be able to have time off. I want to be part of it. I need to feel I'm part of it.'

'How do I know you won't change your mind?'

'I need time to prove that to you. I'm asking you to give me that time. Meet me halfway. Please. I want to be the father of your children,' he pleaded as they stepped out of the lift. 'I'm just asking for a little more time.'

She could give up her dreams of a pregnancy in the near future or she could give up Otto. The decision was hers.

* * *

Lily yawned and stretched. It was good to be busy, it kept her mind off the subject of her ticking biological clock and off babies.

She'd chosen Otto. She didn't want a future without him and she didn't want to have babies without him so she'd chosen her husband and hoped she'd be able to live with the reality of delaying her family. But it was easier said than done.

When she was busy she could block out thoughts of babes and pregnancy but in the long hours of the night she tossed and turned. Her mind was restless and she imagined she could feel her empty womb aching. She was exhausted. Even though Otto slept beside her she was edgy, unable to still the thoughts, and the lack of sleep was making her tired and grumpy. She'd lost her appetite and she was feeling emotionally fragile. This wasn't how things were supposed to be.

She breathed deeply in an attempt to get some oxygen to her brain. The air in the ED felt stagnant and smelt stale. Perhaps she should pop outside while she had a moment, she thought. But before she could stand the phone on the triage desk rang, startling her.

'Incoming patient,' Julie announced, as

she replaced the receiver. 'Male in his twenties, multiple injuries, a fall at Ben Buckler.'

Lily stood up quickly, before her blood pressure could stabilise, and she grabbed at the desk as the room spun around her.

'Are you all right?' Julie asked.

'Yes,' she said as her surroundings steadied. 'Just a bit light-headed. I think I stood up too fast.' The ED had been busy and she'd missed lunch, that wasn't uncommon, so perhaps her fatigue was also having an impact on her blood sugar. She should probably have something to eat but that would have to wait.

The ambulance pulled up and Poppy emerged from the rear. She 'd been back at work for a month since returning from her honeymoon but she hadn't lost that glow of happiness of the newly married. Lily knew that, in contrast to her younger sister, she was looking tired and worn out. She felt, and looked, as if she could use a holiday.

'Patient is unconscious, has multiple fractures and suspected spinal injuries and will need a mental health assessment,' Poppy said. The steep, unforgiving cliffs of Ben Buckler at the northern end of Bondi Beach were a frequent spot for accidents and some deliberate mishaps as well.

Lily started pushing the stretcher into the

ED as Poppy continued her summary but something wasn't right. Lily could see Poppy's lips moving but it sounded as though she were talking underwater.

Her vision was blurry. She squeezed her eyes shut, trying to clear her vision, but when she opened them there were black spots in her view and then the room began to spin.

'Lily? Lily, can you hear me?'

Lily opened her eyes.

'Where am I?' she asked as she realised she was looking up at Poppy. The last thing she remembered was walking into the ED beside the trolley.

'You're in the ED.'

That was good. 'Why am I lying down?' she asked as the ceiling came into focus behind Poppy's head.

'You fainted.'

'Fainted?' She wasn't a fainter. She'd only fainted once before. Her blood sugar must be really low, she thought as she sat up.

'Slowly,' Poppy warned.

'I'm fine. I skipped lunch.'

'Do you want me to get you something to eat?'

The thought of eating made her nauseous. 'No.' She shook her head. Carefully. 'What are you doing here anyway? Shouldn't you be back on the road? And what happened to our patient?'

Poppy shrugged. 'Ajay's taking care of him and I was owed a break. So unless Alex and I get a call out I thought I'd wait here until Otto gets out of Theatre.'

'You told Otto?'

'Why wouldn't I tell Otto?'

'You didn't need to bother him. I'm fine.'

'He's in Theatre anyway.'

Of course he was busy, Lily thought. It was lucky she was fine otherwise what would he do?

'What's going on?' Poppy wanted to know. 'I thought the two of you had sorted things out.'

Lily hadn't been able to bring herself to share the latest dilemma with her sisters. She was still trying to process it herself. 'So did I,' she admitted, 'but it turns out we were both making assumptions about our relationship.'

'Meaning?'

'I thought being back on track meant that we wouldn't get divorced and we'd start a family. Otto thought it meant we wouldn't get divorced and we'd start a family in a couple of years. He did offer to meet me in the middle. He suggested that we start trying to get pregnant in six months instead of next year but I'm still not sure. I get that I can't have children right now without Otto, it's not like I have another man waiting in the wings, I know it would take time to find someone, establish that relationship, before I could have kids, but what if Otto changes his mind? What if he wants to put things off again?'

'You don't trust him to keep his word?'

That was the big question. She wanted to trust him. She had to trust him if they had any hope of a future. But how was she going to do that? 'I'm going round in circles in my head. I'm not sleeping. I'm tired and anxious and confused. I'm not myself.'

'Are you sure it's just emotional stress? What if it's something physically wrong. You just fainted. Do you want me to get Ajay in here? Maybe he should order blood tests?'

'No. I'm sure I'm fine.'

'Could you be pregnant?' Poppy asked.

'Pregnant!'

She was about to say, *Don't be ridiculous. I'm not pregnant*, but was it completely out of the question?

'When was your last period?' Poppy asked. She had to think. Before the conference.

Before Poppy's wedding. She could feel the colour leave her face as she fought back a rising tide of nausea. 'Six weeks ago.'

'I think you should do a test.'

'I can't be pregnant.' As if saying that would make it true.

'Why not?'

'Because Otto isn't ready.'

She knew it was too soon in their rekindled relationship. As if things needed to get any worse!

Otto took the stairs two at a time, burst through the last door and sprinted into the ED.

'Where is she?'

Julie was at the triage desk and her eyes were wide as he raced past her. 'Exam room four,' she called out.

Otto's heart had lodged in his throat the minute he'd received news that Lily had collapsed. He was furious that the information had been withheld from him until after he'd finished operating even though he understood why. He would not have been able to concentrate if he'd been advised earlier and professionally that would not have been acceptable but, personally, if anything happened to Lily, he would be a broken man. As long as she was OK, he would give her anything she wanted, he vowed. Do anything she wanted.

'Lily!'

She was pale but it wasn't the colour of her skin that worried him. It was the look on her face. She looked petrified.

Oh, God. What was wrong? She'd obviously had bad news.

'I'll wait outside.' He hadn't noticed Poppy until she spoke. She looked at Lily and then left the room. Why was she waiting outside? What was she waiting for?

Otto's fear escalated. 'What is it? What's wrong?' He rushed to Lily's side, kissed her cheek and took her hand. If she'd had bad news so quickly it must be terrible. Anything minor would take longer to find.

Lily was trembling.

He sat beside her and wrapped an arm around her shoulders. Was she cold? Frightened? In shock? Where was a doctor? Who was going to tell him what was going on?

'Lily, you're frightening me. Tell me what's wrong.' He knew this was his moment. The moment to show her he was beside her one hundred per cent. His moment to support her in whatever way she needed. 'Whatever it is, we can handle it. Together.'

Her eyes filled with tears and Otto's heart froze in his chest.

'Lily?'

'I'm pregnant.'

'What?' It took him a moment to process what she was saying. It wasn't what he expected. 'Pregnant?'

She nodded.

He laughed. 'Oh, thank God.'

Lily was frowning. 'You're not upset.'

'No. I'm relieved. You looked terrified and I was expecting bad news. Something life-threatening. Pregnancy isn't terminal.'

'Maybe not. But it is permanent.'

'What does that mean?'

'I'm keeping the baby.'

'Of course we are.' He let out a sign of relief. An unexpected pregnancy was nothing compared to all the ailments he'd imagined could have befallen Lily.

Lily frowned. 'Are you sure? You said you weren't ready for children.'

'I know. But the idea was beginning to grow on me.'

'Really?'

He smiled and sat on the edge of the bed. 'Spending the past month with you, and seeing you with your niece and nephew, I began to see what you saw. What our life would look like. Chaotic, disorganised, sure, but also fun and filled with love. I knew I wasn't going to be able to control everything and that's OK. If I've learnt my lesson, I can accept that some things are out of my control. Like how much I love you.' He leant forwards and kissed her. 'I don't need to control everything. I just need you. All that matters is that you're OK. All I could think of after I heard you'd collapsed was that I would do anything, give you anything, as long as you were safe. I couldn't handle losing you but I reckon I can handle a baby.

'Are you sure? You're not going to freak out? You're not going to tell me it's too soon? That we have things to sort out? That you have a career to establish?'

'Lily, I want children with you, I want a family with you, and if it's sooner rather than later then that's OK. I love you and I promise I will be here for you and our children. One hundred per cent. I apologise for being an arse. I was worrying about things that didn't matter, things that could be sorted.'

'Things that could be fixed,' Lily said with a smile.

'Exactly.' He smiled back. 'And that's my speciality. Fixing is not controlling.'

'I'm sorry I doubted you. I assumed I knew what your reaction was going to be.'

'I would do anything for you. I don't want to lose you. I never wanted to lose you. I love you. I always have and I always will. That has never changed.'

'And what if things go wrong?'

'We have to believe that things will be OK, but if they're not then I hope we've learnt something from counselling. We'll talk to each other, support each other. We're going to do this together. Today and every day. We're a team. And this baby will be the newest member. This baby is our future.' Otto put one hand under her chin and tipped her face up so she was looking at him. 'I want you to look at me and see someone who will take care of you and our family. I want you to look at me and see someone who loves you, today and every day. I want you to look at me and see someone who is ready for the next chapter in our life together. Our life as a family. Speaking of which, there is something I've been wanting to discuss with you.'

'Yes?'

'I think we should renew our wedding vows. Make our promises in front of our friends and family as we start the next phase of our life together. What do you think?'

'I think that sounds perfect.'

'And I also thought we could invite your parents.' He paused, waiting to see if Lily had any strong objections, but when she stayed silent, he continued, 'It might be the chance you've been waiting for, the opportunity to build a relationship. Knowing we're about to start our own family might be the catalyst that's needed. What do you say? How does that sound?'

'It sounds like you want to fix something.' She smiled.

'Only with your permission.'

She nodded. 'I think that's a good idea,' she said as she reached for him and took his face in her hands. She pulled him closer and kissed him. 'I love you. And I will tell anyone who wants to hear it and I will happily marry you all over again.'

EPILOGUE

'AN NA WILLOW CARLSON-CHEN! Be careful!' Mei called out to her daughter, who was jumping into the pool, narrowly missing Niki, who was splashing about with Lily's father. Pete had made a good recovery following his brain aneurysm sixteen months earlier. He'd committed to his rehabilitation, working hard to restore his balance and strength, motivated by his desire to get back on a surfboard.

The entire Carlson clan, including Lily's parents, Pete and Goldie, had descended on Poppy and Ryder's new house to celebrate Naming Day for the children.

Lily, Mei and Jet were watching the antics in the pool and Jet was laughing as An Na resurfaced, spluttering. 'Our poor child. She's been lumped with a mouthful of a name.'

'It's all out of love,' Mei said.

An Na had officially been given her auntie Willow's name along with a hyphenated surname. The Carlson siblings had agreed to give any daughters 'Willow' as a middle name, a connection to their sister, Daisy's twin, who had been taken from them too early. Today was a celebration of not only An Na's name but also the baptism ceremonies for Poppy and Ryder's five-week-old son, Teddy, and Lily and Otto's daughter, Posie Willow Sofia Rodgers, who was three months old and had been named for her aunt and paternal grandmother.

Lily looked around the garden at her family, in awe about how much had changed in a year. Two babies, two more weddings—Jet and Mei and Daisy and Ajay had all married—and Poppy and Ryder had bought a house. Lily knew how much that stability meant to Poppy and to see her sister, all her siblings, so happy and settled only added to her own happiness.

'Dad, Dad, come in the pool with me,' An Na instructed and Jet willingly obliged. He was a soft touch for his only daughter. As he said, he came into An Na's life late and had to make up for lost time.

'Are you ready to have more kids?' Lily asked her sister-in-law as she lifted her own daughter from her breast, where she had

been feeding, and listened for the little satisfied burp.

'Not just yet. I've got a few more years
of med school to go along with juggling my
shifts with the ambulance service. I don't
think I can put much more on my plate. I
know there will be a big gap between An
Na and any siblings but she'll have plenty
of cousins.'

Lily found it incredible to think that eighteen months ago the four Carlson siblings
had no children in their lives and now there
were four between them.

'Goldie,' Mei called out to her mother-in-
law. 'Come and sit with Lily. I'll bring the
food out.'

Lily looked up to where Otto and Ryder
were cooking the barbecue and Ajay and
Lily's mother, Goldie, were ferrying plates
from the kitchen to the outdoor table, ready
for lunch. Poppy had gone inside to change
Teddy and Daisy was preparing salads.
There was constant movement between people but there was always someone to talk to
or to lend a hand.

Goldie sat down in the chair vacated by
Mei. 'Can I hold Posie?' she asked and Lily
happily passed her the baby. 'She is so beautiful,' Goldie said.

Lily didn't disagree. Her daughter was divine. Fair haired and dark eyed, just as Lily imagined.

'I wish I could remember how it felt to hold you in my arms when you were a newborn but I am so grateful for the chance to hold my grandbabies,' Goldie said.

It had taken some time but, thanks to Otto and his penchant for fixing things, Lily and her siblings were gradually mending their relationship with their parents. Otto had got the ball rolling when he'd organised a renewal of their wedding vows and invited Pete and Goldie. He had listened to Lily when she'd said she felt they should have invited them the first time around and that invitation had been the catalyst that brought them into their grandchildren's lives.

Pete and Goldie had been young parents themselves, with no experience and no family support. By their own admission they hadn't known what they were doing and Goldie, in particular, had found the weight of responsibility too much. Now they were able to enjoy being grandparents, with all care and no responsibility. It was perfect for them and Lily was enjoying getting to know her parents as people, without expectations.

'How are you?' Goldie asked.

Lily knew it was a loaded question but she kept her answer simple and honest. 'I'm good. Tired but happy.'

'Otto said you're starting to think about going back to work? That seems soon.'

'I won't be going back for a few months but I have to start thinking about childcare.'

'What are your plans for that?'

Lily knew her mother wouldn't be offering to help. Pete and Goldie lived in Byron Bay, an eight-hour drive north of Sydney. They were able to visit for special occasions but not available for regular babysitting and Lily and her siblings were fine with that. They weren't sure they were ready to hand over any major child-minding to their parents; they hadn't exactly been model parents when raising their own family. 'Poppy, Daisy and I are thinking about sharing a nanny for Posie, Ted and Niki, although I'm not sure we've convinced Mrs Singh to share Niki,' she replied, 'and then we'll cover any gaps in our shift work rosters between us.'

'You're very lucky to have the support of each other. If I hadn't had the support of the commune I don't know how I would have managed.'

Until recently Lily hadn't thought her parents had managed at all but she hadn't known the full story. Goldie had run away from home, fallen in love with Pete and had Lily when she was eighteen. She'd then fallen pregnant in rapid succession with Jet and then Poppy and had suffered with undiagnosed postnatal depression after Lily's birth before another bout of depression after Daisy's twin, Willow, had died. Goldie's history went a long way to explaining why she'd always seemed so disconnected from her children's lives but forgiveness was an ongoing thing and the revelations were taking some adjusting to. Lily was getting there sooner than Poppy and Daisy but she was mindful that everyone needed to process things in their own way. Perhaps not all the bridges could be repaired.

Lily knew it was Goldie's history of depression that made her check in on Lily's well-being. She also knew that Otto had been watching her closely for any signs of postnatal depression but Lily knew she was fine. In hindsight, she knew she'd suffered depression after the assault that had caused the loss of her first child but having Posie had been the best thing for her. She hadn't forgotten her first daughter, but Posie and Otto's love had put her back together again.

'Mum, would you be able to make your

salad dressing?' Daisy asked as she approached, reaching her hands out to take the baby. Goldie stood up and passed Posie over as Lily smiled. It was lucky Posie was a placid baby who had no qualms about being passed around.

Holding babies suits you, Lily signed as Daisy took the empty seat. Her youngest sister had always had a Madonna-type soul. *Are you and Ajay talking about babies yet?*

'Ajay would like more children and I'd be happy with that but if it happens it happens and if not,' Daisy said with a shrug, 'I already have everything I wanted. I found my person and he came with a bonus in the shape of Niki. I don't need anything more.'

'Lunch is ready,' Otto said as he joined them. 'Do you want me to put Posie down for a nap?'

'Thank you,' Lily said gratefully. She never minded holding her daughter but even she could admit that it was easier to eat a meal when she wasn't trying to juggle a baby.

Otto lifted Posie from Daisy's lap and snuggled her into his shoulder. Lily never tired of watching him with their daughter. Posie adored her father and he adored her. Like Daisy, Lily had everything she ever wanted although she would happily have another baby. But she had time. Otto wasn't going anywhere and neither was she.

It turned out that Daisy was right, she thought as she stood and kissed first Posie's cheek and then Otto's.

There was only one man for her.

* * * * *